SEA OF FLAMES

Depth Force Thrillers
Book Six

Irving A Greenfield

SAPERE
BOOKS

SEA OF FLAMES

Published by Sapere Books.

24 Trafalgar Road, Ilkley, LS29 8HH,
United Kingdom

saperebooks.com

ISBN: 978-1-80055-883-0

DEATH BLAST

"Target," the SO said. *"Bearing, three two zero degrees. Range, three thousand yards."*

At three thousand yards, Boxer and everyone on board the Neptune *knew that the explosion from a nuclear torpedo would destroy not only the target vessel but the* Neptune *as well.*

Boxer forced the consequences from his mind and keyed the forward torpedo room. "Load and arm —"

Suddenly the Neptune *reeled violently. An explosion ripped the bow open, lifting it above the sandbank. Then the boat settled down into the sand and the stern came out of the water, its props spinning wildly above the surface.*

"Forward torpedo room gone," the DCO reported. "Hull ruptured."

"Roger that," Boxer answered. "All hands, abandon ship… Abandon ship… Abandon ship!"

CHAPTER 1

Boxer keyed the diving officer. "Going to autodive."

"Ten four, Skipper," the DO answered.

Boxer used the controls on the command computer to bring and hold the *Turtle* automatically at periscope depth. "Going to five zero feet," he said.

"Five zero feet," echoed Cowly, his executive officer.

Boxer left the COMCOMP and walked slowly across the bridge to the periscope control station. He was a rangy-built man, with gray eyes and a strong-looking face, most of which was hidden by a pepper-and-salt beard that, though it made him look older than his thirty-five years, also made him look more dignified. He stopped and glanced over at Commander Cynthia Lowe.

She met his eyes and shook her head. "Nothing, Skipper. Even the Libyans are silent."

Boxer nodded. "Keep listening. Maybe De Vargas or one of the other guys will signal us," he said.

"Aye, aye, Skipper," Cynthia answered.

Boxer went to the PCS and, activating the instrument, he adjusted it for night vision.

A green light began to flash on the periscope's control panel.

"Five zero feet," Cowly announced.

"Roger that," Boxer said, placing his eyes against the viewing port. "Weather clear. Sea calm," he reported.

"Moonrise in zero six minutes," Cowly said.

"Roger that," Boxer answered, as he made a quick three-hundred-and-sixty-degree sweep: "Land eighty-four degrees. Range, ten thousand yards."

"Moonrise in zero three minutes," Cowly reported.

"Roger that," Boxer acknowledged. The moon would be full and, in a cloudless Mediterranean sky, very bright. Under such conditions it would be easy for anyone to spot a periscope's wake, even if they weren't looking for it. Not only was the Libyan navy and air force hunting for the *Turtle*, but by now, Boxer had no doubt, several Russian warships had joined the search.

Boxer made another three-hundred-and-sixty-degree sweep. "Nothing," he announced. "Not even lights ashore."

"Zero one minute to moonrise," Cowly said.

Boxer touched the periscope retract control, causing the instrument to slide back into its well. "We'll go ashore at oh four hundred," he said to Cowly. "So far we've been lucky. They may be expecting us, but they don't know we're already here."

"With your permission, Skipper, I'd like to lead the landing party," Cowly said.

"Negative," Boxer answered. "We're all going ashore. We're going to give those Libyans the kind of show they won't forget." He turned toward Sanchez. "I want Morell and I want the bastard alive."

"You'll get him," Sanchez said tightly. "Now or later. I swear you'll get him."

"Now!" Boxer snapped. "I want him now. More than a hundred men are out there. A hundred men from this boat have been killed, wounded, or captured," he shouted, "because that bastard set them up."

Sanchez remained silent.

Boxer went to the COMCOMP and switched on the MC. "All hands… Now hear this… All hands… Now hear this… We're going to attack at oh three thirty… We're going to attack

8

at oh three thirty... All hands will assist when and where needed on deck." He switched off the MC, leaned back, and, closing his eyes, used the fingers of his right hand to rub them. He was beyond being tired; he was as close to being completely exhausted as he had ever been. His body was numb and he felt lightheaded. No mission was without losses, but this one was different. This one so far had cost the entire strike force; for this one the Company had been set up...

Boxer dropped his hand, opened his eyes, and found himself looking at Cynthia. She was standing within arm's reach. Before she'd been assigned to the *Turtle*, they had been lovers now and then. He was more casual about the relationship than she.

"Nothing," she said. "It's as if everyone on shore had dropped off the planet. I don't understand it."

Boxer shrugged. "They might be afraid of an air strike from the fleet. They know it's only a couple of hundred miles from here and they know we're here. By now Morell has probably told them everything they've always wanted to know about the *Turtle*, complete with drawings."

"What a bastard!" she exclaimed.

"Just earning his pay," Boxer answered bitterly. "The life of a double agent is not an easy one."

"Do you think we'll find any of our men?" she asked, looking straight at him.

"I don't know. Honestly, I don't," Boxer answered. "But even if there aren't any of our people there, we'll be able to find out what this boat can really do, won't we?"

"She'll do fine," Cynthia answered confidently. Boxer nodded. "Let's hope she does, or none of us will be around to suggest changes."

"I know she will," Cynthia said.

Boxer nodded and turned his attention back to the COMCOMP. All systems were go. He switched on the MC. "All hands, now hear this… All hands, now hear this… We're heading into shore… We're heading into shore… Gun crews will fire at will… All surface-to-air missiles will be radar-controlled… Surface-to-surface missiles will be fired before we break water… CIC target first two surface-to-surface birds to impact directly behind the cliff… All system-operating stations stand by to go to manual control… Going to manual control."

Boxer switched off the MC and turning to Cowly, he said, "Have Mahony at the helm."

"Aye, aye, Skipper," Cowly answered.

"You stand by the COMCOMP and monitor the UWIS. You and Mahony have to get us up the beach as smoothly as possible."

Cowly nodded, switched on the MC, and said, "Mahony, to the bridge on the double… Mahony, to the bridge on the double."

Boxer faced Cynthia. "I want you to assist the DCO. If we have any serious damage, he'll need all the help he can get."

"Aye, aye, Skipper," she responded and started to leave.

"One more thing," Boxer said.

Cynthia stopped.

Boxer looked straight at her and, remembering the times they had made love, he said in a low voice, "I want you to know that whatever happened between us was my fault, not yours. I just wanted you to know that."

Cynthia flushed. "Thanks for telling me," she whispered. "It means more to me than you'll ever know."

Boxer nodded, then said, "There's one more thing I have to say."

She looked at him questioningly.

"Should we be boarded and overrun, I don't want you to fall into the hands of the enemy. I will try to get to you and…"

"I understand," she answered. "I'll see the Doc before I join the DCO. He'll give me something to do the job. And thank you for being concerned about me in that particular way."

"Let's hope it never comes to that," Boxer said.

She smiled. "Let's hope."

"Mahony, reporting as ordered," Mahony said, coming onto the bridge. He was a wiry-built man with red hair, blue eyes, and freckled face.

Boxer turned his attention to him. "Take the helm. You and Mr. Cowly work as a team."

"Aye, aye, Skipper," Mahoney answered.

"Good luck, Skipper," Cynthia said.

Boxer nodded and turned his attention back to the COMCOMP. All systems were green.

Cowly bent close to the UWIS screen. "Looks like the slope of the beach begins about five zero yards out from the shore," he said.

"The chart has it at eight zero," Boxer said.

For several minutes, neither man spoke; then Boxer asked the SO for a distance check.

"Five thousand yards and closing fast," the SO responded.

Boxer switched on the MC. "All section officers report status," he said.

One by one the second officers responded.

"All sections ready," Boxer told Cowly.

"I'd feel better if going in wasn't so easy," Cowly responded.

Boxer keyed the EO. "Reduce speed to one zero knots."

"Reducing speed to one zero knots," the EO answered.

"Three thousand yards and still closing fast," the SO reported.

"Ten four," Cowly answered; then to Boxer he said, "I'm going to have to switch on the high-intensity lights for the last hundred yards."

"Keep them off as long as possible," Boxer said. "We want to come out of the water with all deck guns in action."

Cowly nodded.

"Two thousand yards and closing fast," the SO said.

"Ten four," Cowly responded. "At one thousand yards stop reporting."

"Ten four," the SO said.

Boxer keyed the EO. "Reduce speed to zero three knots."

"Reducing speed to zero three knots," the EO answered.

Even though the *Turtle*'s internal temperature and humidity were held at optimum levels, Boxer was sweating. He ran his right sleeve across his face.

"One thousand yards," the SO reported.

"Ten four," Cowly answered. "Mahony, hold her steady as she goes."

"Holding steady as she goes," Mahony replied.

Cowly peered at the UWIS screen and pursed his lips. His heart was pounding so loud, he was sure everyone on the bridge could hear it. "Where's the damn beach slope?" he muttered under his breath.

Boxer switched on the MC. "Gun details fire at will as soon as we're out of the water… Pick your targets… There's enough moonlight to make your rounds count." He switched off the MC and checked the boat's operating systems.

The medical officer keyed Boxer. "Skipper, Captain Bush requests permission to be allowed to leave the sick bay and report to the bridge."

For the time being, Boxer had put Bush out of his mind. "Denied," Boxer answered tersely. "Sedate him again."

"What?"

"You heard me… I don't care how you do it, but I want him sedated."

"Aye, aye, Skipper," the MO responded.

"What I don't need now," Boxer commented aloud, "is Captain Bush on the bridge."

Without taking his eyes off the UWIS, Cowly nodded.

Boxer glanced over at Sanchez. The man was very pale. Morell had been one of his men. He had convinced the Company chief, Kinkade, to go for it.

"Beach slope in sight!" Cowly reported. "One hundred yards."

Boxer checked the UWIS. The slope of the beach was a gray incline.

"I'm going to need the lights," Cowly said.

"The moment —"

The SO keyed Boxer. "Target bearing one five degrees… Range, twenty-five thousand yards… Speed, three five knots… ID, OSA-class attack boat."

"Roger that," Boxer said. He was sweating profusely and used the back of his sleeve to wipe his forehead.

"Come to course eight nine degrees," Cowly told Mahony.

"Coming to course eight nine degrees," Mahony answered.

Boxer checked the sonar display screen on the COMCOMP. The target was still twenty-five thousand yards away. "I don't think she's looking for us. Anyway not yet."

"Five zero yards to beach," Cowly reported.

"Roger that," Boxer said, shifting his eyes from the sonar display to the UWIS.

"Stand by to ground," Cowly announced.

Boxer switched on the MC. "All hands, brace yourselves... Standby to ground," he said and, sucking in his breath, he waited for the sound that every sailor dreads...

Within moments, the bottom of the *Turtle*'s bow ground against the slope of the beach. She shivered, rolled slightly to one side, and then her stern settled down.

Boxer activated the tread release and three sets of dual treads came out of the *Turtle*'s hull and gently lifted her two feet off the bottom. Boxer keyed the EO. "Transfer drive power to treads."

"Transferring DP to treads," the EO answered.

The *Turtle* suddenly gave a slight lurch forward and began to move.

"Disconnecting helm," Boxer said, repositioning two switches. "Helmsman, check helm."

"Checking helm," Mahony said. "No response."

"Roger that," Boxer answered.

"Lights," Cowly said.

"Lights," Boxer answered, turning on the *Turtle*'s high-intensity searchlights. The entire underwater slope was brilliantly illuminated.

"They have to know something is down here," Cowly said, looking at the UWIS screen. "Clear ahead."

Boxer increased the *Turtle*'s speed to two miles an hour. He switched on the MC. "Going to night lighting," he said. An instant later the *Turtle*'s lighting changed from white to red.

"Surface on the screen," Cowly said.

"Stand by," Boxer said, on the MC. "All hands stand by... We're breaking water... We're breaking water."

Boxer switched off the MC and bolted for the topside bridge. Cowly held the *Turtle* on her course up the beach.

"Missiles away," the fire control officer announced.

Boxer was at the exterior COMCOMP. "Roger that," he said.

An instant later four explosions tore the top of the cliff off.

The deck guns opened fire.

Boxer keyed Cowly. "Report to the bridge," he said.

"Ten four," Cowly answered.

Boxer drove the *Turtle* up the beach and turned her to the right.

Cowly joined him. "Looks like we caught them by surprise," he shouted.

"Looks like it," Boxer answered.

"If any of our men are — Christ!"

Boxer saw the poles the same instant. There were fifty or more of them upright in the sand; on each a man was impaled.

One of the junior officers on the bridge began to vomit.

"Could any of them be alive?" Cowly asked.

"Maybe," Boxer answered. "But —" He stopped and shook his head. "No," he said tightly. "They're either dead or dying."

The ground exploded into a dark plume on their port side.

Boxer keyed the forward deck gun. "Knock out that gun," he said.

"Aye, aye, Skipper," the Section Chief answered.

"Where's the Lieutenant?" Cowly asked.

"Should be in those rocks. About two hundred yards from us," Boxer answered.

A round slammed into the *Turtle*. She took it without a quiver.

"Tanks, on the stern," one of the junior officers shouted.

Boxer keyed the MO. "Stand by to launch your birds... Four tanks coming at us from the stern."

"Aye, aye, Skipper."

Boxer keyed the RO. "Lock on land targets at bearing six seven degrees and feed info to SMS battery."

"Aye, aye, Skipper," the RO answered.

"I see the rocks!" Cowly exclaimed. "They're close to the water's edge."

Changing the speed of the treads, Boxer turned the *Turtle* toward the rocks.

The RO keyed Boxer. "Bogies... Bearing one four five degrees... Altitude four thousand feet... Speed two hundred knots... Range five miles... Closing fast."

"Roger that," Boxer answered.

The surface-to-surface missiles roared away. A few moments later the four tanks dissolved into a huge ball of fire that continued to move forward, faltered, then came to a stop.

Boxer switched on the MC. "Deck detail... Deck detail topside... De Vargas, make it to our port side... Make it to our port side... We'll cover you."

The RO keyed Boxer. "Bogies closing fast."

"Roger that," Boxer said.

Another moment passed and the surface-to-air missiles were away.

Three explosions hammered down on the beach and three balls of fire fell into the sea.

Cowly swept the rocks with the searchlights.

"We can't stay here very long," Boxer said, bringing the *Turtle* to a stop.

Suddenly a round exploded over the *Turtle*.

"Medic," someone shouted from the machine-gun section. "Medic to the machine-gun section."

Two men came out of the hull and ran along the deck.

"There's the Lieutenant!" Cowly shouted. "There he is!"

"Deck detail... Survivors port side!" Boxer said over the MC. "Survivors on the port side... I didn't think anyone would make it," Boxer said, watching the deck detail lift De Vargas and six other men aboard. "Not after seeing those poles."

"Morell is with them," Cowly said.

"I see him," Boxer answered.

The section chief keyed Boxer. "That's it... There's no one else left... Everyone else has been killed or captured."

"Roger that," Boxer said. "Get De Vargas and his men below."

"Aye, aye, Skipper," the officer answered.

Boxer put the *Turtle* in motion again. "I'm going straight for the water. We've been lucky so far and I don't want to stretch it."

Cowly nodded.

The *Turtle* moved down the beach slowly toward the water.

Suddenly De Vargas keyed Boxer. "Skipper, there's a fuckin' minefield out there... Either you go out the way you came in, or you keep going down the beach about a thousand yards; then head out to sea."

"Roger that, Lieutenant," Boxer answered. "Did I say something about luck?" he asked.

Cowly nodded and then asked, "Do we go back the way we came in, or —"

"We'll go for the end run," Boxer said, turning the *Turtle* up the beach.

The RO keyed Boxer. "Multiple targets... Bearings zero nine, one zero, one five and one nine degrees... Target speed three five knots... Range twenty thousand yards... All targets ID the same."

"Roger that," Boxer replied; then to Cowly he said, "We must get to the bottom before those MTBs reach us."

Cowly was about to answer when an explosion burst on the *Turtle*'s stern. She shuddered but continued to move forward.

Boxer keyed the DCO. "Any problems?" he asked.

"Negative," the DCO answered.

Boxer switched on the MC. "De Vargas, report to the bridge... De Vargas, report to the bridge."

The RO keyed Boxer. "Four tanks, midship, on the starboard side, Skipper."

"Roger that," Boxer said and keyed the two gunnery officers. "Tanks on the starboard side," he told them.

"Got them on the scope," the forward-deck gun officer responded.

"On the scope," the stern-deck gun officer said.

The two guns went off simultaneously.

One of the tanks burst into flames. Another lurched to the left, flipped over on its side, and began to burn.

Suddenly, three explosions smashed down on the *Turtle*. She tipped to the starboard side, then righted herself, and continued to lumber up the beach.

"Report casualties," Boxer said over the MC.

"None," the forward deck GO answered.

"Negative," the aft GO reported.

"Everyone is okay," the machine-gun section chief said.

"Skipper," De Vargas said, "their aim is getting better."

"We can't risk hitting a mine," Boxer said, guessing what De Vargas was thinking.

"There's got to be a way through the minefield," De Vargas said.

Two more rounds slammed into the *Turtle*'s starboard side.

The DCO keyed Boxer. "We've got a ruptured hydraulic line," he said.

"To where?"

"Lift mechanism for the SAM launcher," the DO answered.

"Roger that," Boxer answered.

"Morell might know where the path is?" De Vargas suggested.

"I wouldn't trust him —"

The RO keyed Boxer. "MTBs six thousand yards and closing fast... On same headings."

"Roger that," Boxer answered. "We get caught in a minefield with those bastards over us and we're dead."

Before De Vargas could answer, the RO keyed Boxer again. "Ten bogies, bearing two seven eight degrees... Altitude, nine thousand feet... Range, thirty miles... Speed, two five zero knots."

"Roger that," Boxer answered.

"We're not going to be able to take them all out," Cowly said.

Boxer keyed the COMMO. "Send the following to Shield. Need air cover at once. Heading for your protection... Keep sending this under a code ten priority."

"Aye, aye, Skipper," COMMO answered.

The SAM section chief keyed Boxer. "Ready to fire."

"Fire at will," Boxer said.

"Ten four, Skipper," the section chief answered.

The next moment the missiles roared away.

Boxer watched the planes take evasive action.

Two became balls of fire and two more started to fall, leaving trails of black smoke behind them.

Boxer switched on the MC. "Stand by, all hands... Stand by, all hands... We're going to —"

The first missile slammed into the beach just ahead of the *Turtle*. The explosion threw up a dark curtain of sand and rock that came crashing down on the deck.

"That crater will trap us!" Boxer shouted, turning the *Turtle* toward the sea.

Another missile crashed into the forward gun turret, ripping it apart. Three secondary explosions followed.

Over the MC Boxer called, "DC on deck... Fire forward deck gun... DC on deck... All medics on deck... Forward gun deck... All medics to forward gun deck."

Two more missiles crashed into the beach close to the *Turtle*.

"Ten yards to the water," Cowly exclaimed. "Ten fucking yards."

Boxer hit the klaxon twice. "All hands clear the deck... All hands clear the deck... Prepare to dive."

"We'll need at least fifty feet of water," Cowly said.

"You and De Vargas get below. I'll stay topside until we can dive," Boxer said.

Cowly looked at De Vargas. "You've had it —"

De Vargas shook his head.

"Request permission to remain on bridge," De Vargas said.

The MO keyed Boxer. "No one survived in the forward gun deck section."

"Roger that," Boxer answered.

"Request permission to remain on bridge," Cowly said.

"Permission denied. Now, the two of you get off the bridge," Boxer shouted. "And I mean *now!*"

Cowly and De Vargas clambered down the open hatch.

The RO keyed Boxer. "Surface craft two thousand yards away... Bogies on —"

"Secure surface radar," Boxer said.

"Aye, aye, Skipper," the RO answered.

Boxer watched the bow of the *Turtle* nose into the water. To gain diving room it would need at least fifty feet. She'd handle like a ship again in thirty feet of water but needed at least fifty to run submerged. And he was going to take her straight down!

Six fighter bombers were streaking toward the *Turtle*. The roar of their engines seemed to eat up the sky.

A salvo of twelve missiles came at the *Turtle*. The explosions slashed into her. She faltered, trembled, and lurched forward. Moments later tons of water and debris crashed down on her deck.

The DCO keyed Boxer. "Main water supply evaporator damaged... Secondary power supply out."

"Can the units be repaired?" Boxer asked.

"Will try," the DCO answered.

"Roger that," Boxer answered.

The deck was almost awash.

Boxer keyed Cowly. "Put Mahony on the helm... You take the UWIS. I want Morell on the bridge by the time I get there."

"Aye, aye, Skipper," Cowly answered.

Boxer checked the position of the MTBs; he guessed they were about two thousand yards away. He keyed the EO. "I need more power on the treads," he said.

"No can give, Skipper... You've all but burned out the bearings as it is."

Boxer shook his head and keyed the COMMO. "Send a message to Shield... Tell them the sky has fallen."

"Aye, aye, Skipper," the COMMO said.

Boxer saw the planes climb, wheel, and come streaking in from the sea for the attack. In a matter of minutes — four or five at the most — the *Turtle* would be underwater.

Suddenly the planes roared a few feet off the surface of the sea and then climbed to leap over the cliff.

For a few moments Boxer was too surprised to think. He had expected to be dead, but he wasn't, and the *Turtle* was still lumbering down into the water. He looked toward the open sea. The MTBs had hove to. He turned toward the cliff. The planes were just coming over it. "We were too damn close to them," Boxer said aloud. "Too close to allow those bastards to fire." He grinned.

The COMMO keyed Boxer. "Skipper, Shield is just over the horizon… Help should be here within seconds."

"Roger that," Boxer said. "We can use all the help we can get."

Boxer checked the water. It was halfway up the sail.

The COMMO keyed Boxer again. "Skipper, the commander of the MTB squadron has asked to speak to you."

"What?"

"He's on a priority one frequency."

"Patch him through," Boxer growled.

"Captain Boxer," his counterpart said in perfect English, "I am asking for your surrender."

"Surrender!" Boxer exclaimed, too surprised to respond any other way.

"I give you my word that no harm will come to you or your crew."

Boxer keyed the forward TO. "Ready three fish," he said in a low voice. "All setting on manual… Fire on manual."

"Aye, aye, Skipper."

"Captain," the squadron commander said, "you have two minutes to make up your mind before I order our planes to blow you out of the water."

"I am considering your offer," Boxer answered.

"A wise move," the officer said.

Boxer switched on the *Turtle*'s short-range radar; then keyed the TO. "Targets, bearing eight nine degrees, eight five degrees, and eight zero degrees... Range two thousand two zero zero yards... Set time distance fuse... Fire at will."

"Aye, aye, Skipper," the TO answered.

"Captain, you have —"

A sudden scream of jet engines came from the direction of the sea.

An instant later a half-dozen F-42s were in swirling combat with the Libyan fighters.

The MTBs started their engines.

The TO keyed Boxer. "Fish away," he reported.

"Roger that," he answered, glancing up at the sky that was filled with the roar of fighter planes and streaking missiles.

Then suddenly three explosions turned the MTBs into balls of orange flames.

"That's for all the guys on the beach," Boxer said grimly, as the orange gave way to the black smoke of burning oil.

The TO keyed Boxer. "Did we get them?" he asked.

"All three," Boxer answered.

"Ten four," the TO said.

Boxer looked down at the water. It was no more than a couple of inches from the lip of the bridge. He secured the command console, dropped through the hatchway, and dogged the hatch shut after him. Moments later he was on the *Turtle*'s main bridge.

CHAPTER 2

Boxer stood at the COMCOMP. His eyes moved back and forth between the overhead depth gauge and the UWIS screen. The *Turtle* was inching slowly into deeper water and inexorably toward her death in the minefield.

"Morell!" Boxer snapped out.

Morell remained silent.

Boxer turned. "I called you, mister," he said, facing the man.

"I heard you, Captain," Morell answered.

"Either you come forward," Boxer said, "or I'll have you dragged here."

Morell hesitated, then moved toward the COMCOMP.

"We're going straight for a minefield," Boxer said.

"That's your problem, Captain."

Boxer's fisted right hand crashed into Morell's jaw.

The man staggered.

"That's not the kind of answer I want to hear," Boxer said.

Morell rubbed his chin. "I'm a prisoner of war —"

"You're not even here," Boxer said, "unless I say you are. Now listen to me, Morell. Listen real good. Either you tell me what I want to know, or I'll have you stuffed into a torpedo tube and fired."

Morell shook his head. "I'm a dead man no matter what I do."

"Four five feet," Cowly said.

Boxer looked over his shoulder at the depth gauge. The needle crept up to fifty.

"Time is running out," Boxer said, facing Morell.

"And what do I get for saving —"

"You bastard," Boxer exploded. "You fucking bastard… You're responsible for the deaths of a hundred men and you want to bargain with me for your miserable life!"

"It's my life."

"You don't — "

"I have a royal flush. This boat and the lives of everyone aboard is in my hands. Without my help —"

"What do you want?"

"To be put ashore on Sardinia or, better still, Sicily."

"Minefield dead ahead," Cowly said.

Boxer turned to the COMCOMP and keyed the EO. "Stop all engines."

"All engines stopped," the EO said.

The *Turtle* came to an abrupt halt.

Boxer looked at the UWIS. The image of the minefield stretched across the screen.

"I hold the cards," Morell said.

Boxer nodded. "You hold the cards," he said. "I'll have you put ashore."

"Where?"

"Sicily," Boxer said, facing Morell.

Boxer glanced at Cowly, then at De Vargas. Neither man's face gave any indication of what he was thinking.

"One life for everyone aboard and — "

"Ashore in Sicily," Boxer said with a nod.

Morell moved toward the UWIS. "The channel through the field is off to the right, at approximately seventy-nine degrees."

"Where the MTBs were!" Boxer exclaimed. "I should have guessed."

Morell shrugged. "A deal is a deal," he said.

Boxer ignored him and keyed the DO. "Bring her to three zero feet."

"Aye, aye, Skipper," the DO answered.

"Anything else I should know about the field?" Boxer asked, annoyed at himself for not having guessed where the channel was.

"The field is less than half a mile deep. But it runs for several miles up the beach."

Boxer nodded and keyed the EO. "Zero five knots."

"Zero five knots," the EO answered.

Boxer turned to Cowly. "Bring her to seven nine degrees."

"Seven nine degrees," Cowly said to Mahony.

Mahony repeated the new heading and eased the wheel over.

In a matter of minutes, the *Turtle* was making its way through the channel toward the open sea.

The COMMO keyed Boxer. "Skipper, message from flight CO."

"Read it."

"Unless otherwise directed by you, flight will return to Shield."

"Send the following... Make a quick recon of area... Use cliffs as center point... Cover an arc of one eight zero degrees running in an east-west direction... Use a radius of one zero zero miles."

The COMMO repeated the message.

"Send it," Boxer said.

"Aye, aye, Skipper," the COMMO answered.

Boxer checked the SYSNET. All operating systems were go.

"End of field in sight," Cowly reported.

Boxer checked the UWIS. Directly ahead of the *Turtle* lay the open sea. "Looks good," he said to Cowly.

"Damn good, Skipper," Cowly answered.

Boxer checked the fathometer. "Another one zero feet of water under us," he told Cowly.

"The more the better," Cowly grinned.

Boxer left the COMCOMP and went to the periscope station, activated the instrument, and made a quick three-hundred-and-sixty-degree search. "No activity," he reported and lowered the periscope into its well.

COMMO keyed him. "Skipper, Shield squadron leader reports two *Sovremenny* class destroyers nine five miles to the east. Moving at three zero knots."

"Roger that," Boxer answered. "Give squadron leader my thanks and tell him to return to Shield base."

"Aye, aye, Skipper," the COMMO answered.

Boxer keyed the DO. "Coming into deep water... Prepare to make one zero zero feet."

"Aye, aye, Skipper," the DO answered.

"Through minefield," Cowly announced.

Boxer nodded and, turning to De Vargas, he said "Get some rest. We'll talk later."

De Vargas nodded and, looking at Morell, he said in a flat, tired voice, "I should have let those bastards grab you and ram a pole up your ass."

Morell turned away.

"If I didn't think you wanted him," De Vargas said to Boxer, "I would have killed him myself."

Boxer put his arm over De Vargas's shoulders. "Get cleaned up. Eat some hot chow and get some sleep."

De Vargas nodded and left the bridge.

Boxer looked at the fathometer. There was ninety feet of water below them. He keyed the DO. "Make one five zero feet."

"Aye, aye, Skipper," the DO answered.

Boxer switched on the MC. "All hands... All hands... Now hear this... Now hear this... A job well done... Stand down from battle stations." And switching off the MC, he keyed the EO. "Give me thirty knots."

"Thirty knots," the EO answered.

Boxer looked at Cowly. "How about breakfast?" he asked.

"Sounds good to me," Cowly answered.

Boxer placed Morell in the custody of two armed sailors. "If he so much as moves from where you want him," Boxer said, "shoot him. Do you understand?"

"Yes, Skipper," one man answered.

"What about you," Boxer asked the other man. "Do you understand?"

"Yes," the man answered with a nod.

"Then escort him off the bridge and take him to the rear of the mess area. No one — and I mean no one other than myself and Mr. Cowly — is to come anywhere near him."

"Aye, aye, Skipper," the men answered in unison.

Boxer turned to Sanchez. "Would you like to join Cowly and myself for breakfast?" he asked.

"No thanks, Skipper. I don't think my stomach could hold anything down," Sanchez said.

"I understand," Boxer said and, looking at one of the junior officers on the bridge, he said, "Mr. Lamont. You have the CONN. Our heading is one one degrees."

"Aye, aye, Skipper," Lamont answered, after he cleared his throat.

"After breakfast, I'll be in my quarters," Boxer said.

Lamont nodded.

"I'm starved," Boxer said, motioning to Cowly. "What about you?"

"Starved," Cowly answered.

Over coffee Boxer said, "In a few days we'll be home and I'm going to take a vacation. Go somewhere —"

"Skipper, it never works that way," Cowly told him. "At least it doesn't for me. I was going to fly down to Miami for a few days and then go to Santa Fe to see my folks, but here I am in the middle of the Med."

"Mind if I join you?" Cynthia asked.

"Please," Boxer said, gesturing to an empty place on the table bench.

"I'm glad we were able to get some of our men back," she said, picking up bits of ham and egg with her chopsticks.

"Six in all," Boxer said; then he added in a much lower voice, "It cost us more than that to do it."

Cynthia nodded and looked down at her food.

"Sometimes it works that way," Cowly said softly. "We're lucky to be here."

She raised her eyes. "I know that," she answered in a low voice. "But —"

"We did the best we could," Cowly said. "And that's the important thing to remember. That and the fact that we survived."

"Have all your missions been like this one?" she asked, looking at Boxer.

"This one cost us more men," he answered. "But it wasn't any more dangerous than any of the other ones."

She shook her head. "I never really understood what you went through each time you went out."

"How could you?" Cowly said. "I don't believe even Kinkade has any real idea, or for that matter, neither does the admiral."

Boxer finished his coffee and, excusing himself, he stood up. "I need some sack time. The two of you had better get some, yourselves."

Cowly nodded.

"I'll have plenty of time to sleep on the trip home," Cynthia said. "Right now I'm more wide awake than I have ever been."

"I know the feeling," Boxer said with a smile and he left the table.

Cowly followed him with his eyes. "There's not a better skipper in the service," he said.

"Even though we had a different relationship, I think I realized that even before I came aboard," Cynthia answered.

Cowly took out a pack of cigarettes, offered her one, held the lighter for her, and then lit his own. Suddenly he realized that he was going to do something that he had been thinking about doing for several days. His heart began to race. "I have something to ask you," he said, blowing smoke off to the left. "When we reach port, would you — I mean — I… Would you spend a few days with me. We could go up to New York and take in a few shows, or go to any other place you'd like." He stopped and, before she could answer, he said, "I'm sorry I didn't mean to —"

"Yes," Cynthia answered. "Yes. I'll go with you. But —"

"But what?" Cowly asked.

"Usually a man invites a woman on a date before he asks her to sleep with him."

Cowly flushed, looked around, and said, "I'm sorry, but I guess I thought because of what we already shared, we —"

"I understand," Cynthia told him. "I feel the same way."

"Do you?"

"I wouldn't have said 'yes,' if I didn't," she answered.

Cowly wanted to reach out and touch her hand, but instead, he smiled at her and said, "Thanks."

She smiled back at him and nodded.

Awake, Boxer lay in his bunk. According to the time on the digital clock above his desk, he had been asleep for a half-hour. Not nearly as long as he had thought and not nearly as long as he should have had, but he would have time enough to sleep once the *Turtle* was back in Norfolk.

An officer on the bridge keyed him. "Skipper, Mr. Morell requests permission to speak to you."

"Permission denied," Boxer snapped.

"Aye, aye, Skipper," the officer answered.

"Belay that," Boxer said, changing his mind. "Have him brought to my quarters."

"Aye, aye, Skipper."

Boxer reached over to the dimmer control and brightened the overhead light; then he sat up, rubbed his eyes, and, taking a pipe from the rack on the shelf over his bunk, he filled the bowl with fresh tobacco. A few moments later, he was smoking contentedly.

A sharp knock on the door drew his attention to it. "Come in," he said.

The door opened and a sailor said, "Mr. Morell is here, Skipper."

Boxer nodded. "Stand by outside."

"Aye, aye, Skipper," the sailor answered and stepped aside to let Morell enter Boxer's quarters.

"Close the door," Boxer said.

Morell nodded and closed the door.

Boxer stood up, went to the desk, and, pointing to the chair next to him, said, "Sit down."

"I'd rather stand."

"I said 'sit down.'"

"As you wish," Morell answered.

Boxer puffed hard on his pipe before he asked, "Do you know what was done to my men back there on the beach?"

"I was there, remember?"

"There must be more to this than just a simple double cross," Boxer said.

Morell remained silent.

"I could use drugs to find out —"

"But you don't have the time," Morell finished for him. "Besides, you don't want to get inside of my brain."

"I only want to know about this mission."

"What you saw —"

"I wasn't on the beach," Boxer said. "De Vargas was."

"Good man, that Lieutenant of yours. One of the best I have ever seen. Had to be to take me."

Boxer frowned. "This mission is going to shake a few trees in Washington."

"Kinkade knew that when he authorized it," Morell answered.

Boxer nodded. "You're probably right about that. But —"

"I will tell you nothing," Morell said. "Absolutely nothing."

Boxer could feel himself becoming angrier and angrier. Morell was a pro and, short of using drugs on him, he'd reveal nothing. "In a few hours we'll be off Sicily," he said.

"Four at the most," Morell answered confidently.

"Do you have a particular place where you want to be put ashore?"

Morell shook his head. "Any place will do. I have friends everywhere on the island."

"You don't have any aboard this boat," Boxer snapped.

Morell shrugged. "A man can't have everything now, can he?"

"Morell, I don't know what you are, but you're not a man. Not by a long shot."

"Don't really care what you or, for that matter, what anyone thinks about me. I'm good at what I do."

"If you're so damn good," Boxer exploded, "why the hell are you here?"

A hint of a smile played across Morell's lips, but he said nothing.

"Guards," Boxer called.

The door swung open and two sailors appeared.

"Escort him back to the holding area," Boxer said.

In the fading late-afternoon light Trish and Borodine walked hand in hand along the Potomac River. A cold northeast wind made the water choppy.

"I don't know how to deal with this," Trish said, her breath steaming in the cold air. She stopped suddenly. "I don't — I shouldn't even be here."

"Then why did you come?" Borodine asked. He was a broad-shouldered man, with a pepper-and-salt beard and sideburns. He spoke English with a distinct Russian accent.

Trish shook her head but didn't answer. After their first dinner date, she swore to herself that she'd never see him again alone, but he had called her two days later and had asked her to go to a concert with him at the Kennedy Center. She had agreed and after that they had continued to meet several times a week.

Borodine raised her gloved hand to his lips and kissed it.

"Don't," she said.

"All right, I won't," he answered. Then he added, "Boxer has been in a fierce action."

Trish stopped again and looked up at Borodine.

"He's safe. But —"

"But what?" she asked, her voice rising.

"Many of the men from the strike force were killed," he told her.

Trish took a deep breath and exhaled slowly. "I hate what he does," she said tightly. "And sometimes I hate him for doing it." She began to walk. "And being with you doesn't make it easier. It makes me feel cheap."

"I'm sorry it does that," Borodine said.

Trish opened her bag and rummaged for a pack of cigarettes. "I can never find what I want, when I want it," she said irritably.

"Permit me," Borodine said, holding an opened cigarette case in front of her.

She took a cigarette. "Not Russian, I hope," she said.

"American," Borodine answered, lighting her cigarette. Then taking one for himself, he let it stay in the right corner of his lips.

"You too are in the same deadly business," she said fiercely. "The same bloody business."

"Now I am in Washington," Borodine answered.

"But you can't wait to get back to sea, can you? Be honest. Wouldn't you rather be at sea?"

"Now — this moment — I'd rather be with you. I'd rather make love to you than do anything else. I'd rather be in bed with you than be anywhere else."

Trish flicked her cigarette into the river. "I'm cold," she said petulantly. "I want to go back to the car."

Borodine nodded and, sniffing the air, he said, "I think there will be snow by morning."

Trish didn't answer.

Borodine opened the door for her and then slid behind the wheel. The car belonged to Trish, but, whenever he was with her, he drove.

"Home?" he asked.

"I was recently divorced from one man," Trish said, turning toward him. "And Jack and I are lovers."

"I didn't ask for an explanation of —"

"My grandfather is head of the CIA," she said. "His people might be following us now."

"No one has followed us," Borodine said quietly. "Not even any agents from the KGB."

"Our situation is completely impossible!" she exclaimed.

"If you think so," Borodine answered, putting the key in the ignition.

"Now you're angry," Trish said. "I can tell by the sound of your voice."

"Why did you agree to meet me?" Borodine asked.

"Because — because I wanted to be with you," Trish admitted.

He turned toward her. "Then be with me! Make love with me!"

"And afterward?" Trish asked in a low voice. "What happens afterward? It's not as if we could have some sort of life together. Could you imagine what would happen if you married me?"

"How can I answer that?"

Borodine lit a cigarette and gave it to Trish.

"Thanks," she said.

He lit one for himself and lowered the window a bit. "I was not thinking of marrying —"

"I know that," she answered, blowing a stream of smoke toward the windshield. "I was just supposing."

"My command would be taken away from me," Borodine said. "Perhaps, I'd be made to resign from the navy."

"I understand."

Borodine shook his head. "No, you don't understand. Here you don't have the same rules."

"My grandfather would go into a screaming orbit if he found out I was seeing you."

Borodine laughed. "I like that."

"What?"

"'Screaming orbit,'" he said. "I never heard that before."

Trish stubbed out her cigarette in the dashboard ashtray. "Let's go."

Borodine buckled his safety belt, turned on the ignition, and released the handbrake. Putting the shift in reverse, he backed out of the parking slot.

Trish put her hand on his. "I don't want to go home," she whispered.

Borodine glanced at her.

She nodded.

Boxer was at the periscope. He scanned a small cove with a small sandy beach. "How long till sundown?" he asked.

"Three to five minutes," Cowly answered, checking the COMCOMP.

Boxer touched the PC button and the periscope slid into its well. "We'll lie off the coast until an hour after sunset," he said, returning to the COMCOMP. "Then we'll surface and put Morell ashore."

"Are we going in —"

"Negative. He goes in on a rubber assault boat," Boxer said.

"Who goes with him?"

"I haven't decided that yet," Boxer answered, lighting his pipe.

The medical officer keyed Boxer. "Captain Bush is asking for you," he said. "He wants to speak with you."

"Roger that," Boxer answered. "Tell him I'll be with him in a short while."

"He wants permission to go to the bridge."

"Negative."

"Ten four," the MO answered.

Boxer turned to Cowly and motioned him closer. "I'm going to have Morell taken out," he said calmly.

"Shouldn't you check —"

Boxer waved the suggestion aside. "Langley wouldn't have the guts to take any action against one of their own."

"Not even after what happened?"

"There would be an investigation, sure. But Kinkade would have to protect the man. He'd have to since this operation was his idea."

"Who's going to do it?" Cowly asked.

"Sanchez," Boxer said. "Only he doesn't know it yet. Morell was his man."

Cowly nodded.

"I'll send one of De Vargas's men and Sanchez ashore with Morell," Boxer explained. "But Sanchez will be the one to take Morell out."

"Are you sure —"

"Yes," Boxer answered. "Morell must never be allowed to play his games again and the only way to stop him from playing is to kill him."

"Skipper, that makes you the judge and the jury."

Boxer nodded. "No. The guys we left on the beach are the jury. And yes, I'm the judge."

"Who do you want to go?"

"I'd send De Vargas, but he'd do the job himself and that's not who I want to do it. Any one of the men who came back. Any one of them. Make it seem like a routine assignment."

"Will do," Cowly answered.

Boxer puffed on his pipe for several moments, sending a column of smoke toward the low ceiling. Then he said, "Take the CONN and have Sanchez report to me in my quarters."

"Aye, aye, Skipper," Cowly said.

The motel was in Virginia. The room was decorated in colonial motif and, in the demilight of early morning, it looked almost unreal to Borodine. There was nothing in Russia that it could be compared to, except perhaps an inn, but even that comparison was inadequate, as was any he could make between the woman sleeping next to him and any other woman with whom he had made love. He could easily fall in love with this woman...

"Are you awake?" Trish asked.

"Yes," Borodine answered, turning toward her. She smelled of sleep and perfume.

Trish put her hand on his bare shoulder. "We slept the night through."

"It was a good sleep," he said.

"A very good one," she added and kissed his chest. "I wish we didn't have to go."

"I must report to the embassy."

"I know. I know you must."

Borodine moved his hand through her long blond hair. "There are so many things I want to say to you, but I only know the words in Russian."

"You knew enough English last night," she teased.

"Ah, but what I did didn't require —"

"Will you do what you did again?" she asked, pressing her naked body against his.

He kissed her.

As soon as the *Turtle* surfaced, Boxer opened the hatch and took his position on the bridge. Cowly was next to him. Neither of them spoke.

At the base of the sail, on the starboard side, a door swung open. Sanchez, Morell, and Thomas Ryan, a man from De Vargas's assault team, came out on deck.

"I'd feel a lot better, if there wasn't a full moon," Boxer commented, looking up at the white disk that was about fifteen degrees above the horizon.

"How much did you tell Ryan?" Cowly asked in a whisper.

"Only that Morell has to be killed."

"Any reaction?"

"He volunteered to do it," Boxer answered.

Cowly nodded. "So would any of the men who came back," he said. Boxer keyed the EO. "Stop all engines."

"Stopping all engines, Skipper," the EO responded.

The *Turtle* began to lose headway.

Cowly switched on the infrared scope and placing his eyes against the eyepiece, he made a careful three-hundred-and-sixty-degree sweep. "All clear," he said. "But in this light we're visible for miles."

Boxer nodded and looked toward the boat's stern. The white wake was rapidly diminishing.

Ryan keyed him. "Ready to launch," he reported.

"Roger that," Boxer answered. "Stand by to launch as soon as we're dead in the water."

"Aye, aye, Skipper… Standing by."

Boxer checked his watch. It was 1723:10.

"We're dead in the water," Cowly said.

Boxer looked down toward the deck. The inflatable was already in the water. A few moments later, Morell settled in the bow. Then Sanchez sat midship and Ryan took his place in the stern, where he controlled a small outboard engine.

As soon as the inflatable drifted clear of the *Turtle*, the outboard coughed a couple of times before it started up.

"Heading for the beach," Ryan reported.

"Roger that," Boxer answered. Turning to Cowly, he said, "The rest of this is up to Sanchez."

"Do you think Morell has any idea he's in danger?" Cowly asked.

Boxer shrugged. "Even if he has, he has to play out the hand I gave him. I didn't give him any other choice."

Suddenly the inflatable veered off to the left.

"Trouble!" Cowly exclaimed.

The inflatable swung violently to the right.

Boxer keyed Ryan. "What the hell is going on?"

"Skipper, Morell went over the side," Ryan answered.

"What?"

"The bastard went over the side."

"Can you get him?"

"Negative, Skipper. But Sanchez thinks he winged him."

"Winged him!" Boxer exclaimed in disgust. "I wanted that fucker dead."

"Do you want us to search —"

"Negative. Return."

"Aye, aye, Skipper," Ryan said.

Boxer turned to Cowly. "The sonofabitch got away."

Cowly didn't answer.

CHAPTER 3

Boxer sat at the COMCOMP. That Morell was able to escape put him in a dark, angry mood.

Even Cowly, who usually could approach him regardless of the situation, kept a respectful distance between them.

Suddenly Boxer keyed the COMMO. "Send a priority ten message to Langley."

"Copying," the COMMO responded.

"This date... Attempted execution of Bruno Morell failed. Morell is in Sicily. Have your people find and take him out... That's it. Close with the usual."

"Do you want me to read the message back?"

"Negative."

"Aye, aye, Skipper," the COMMO said.

Boxer turned to Cowly. "Now that that's done, I feel a hell of a lot better. I want that bastard Morell dead. I don't want him to ever be in a position to set other guys up."

With a vigorous nod, Cowly agreed, then said, "But I think you're better off letting Kinkade take care of it, than —"

"No. That kind of thing you're better off doing yourself. I gave it to someone else to do. I should have done it myself."

"Are you blaming —"

"No one but myself," Boxer said. "And that's the hardest type of blame to shoulder."

"I know what you mean about that," Cowly replied.

Boxer faced the COMCOMP and checked the *Turtle*'s position. "We should be close to the Shield's destroyer screen."

"We'll reach the edge of their sonar in about three or five minutes," Cowly said.

Boxer keyed the COMMO. "Contact Admiral Bozamato on the *Shiloh* and patch the call through to me."

"Aye, aye, Skipper," the COMMO responded.

"As soon as I finish this call, I'll see Bush," Boxer said.

"What will happen to him?" Cowly asked.

Boxer shrugged. "I don't really know. He needs a great deal of psychiatric help."

The COMMO keyed Boxer. "Admiral Bozamato is on the phone."

"Roger that," Boxer said, picking up the phone. "Thanks for the help, Admiral. It came at the right time and the right place."

"Hear you had some trouble," Bozamato said.

"That's an understatement," Boxer replied. "Sometime, when we can relax over a few drinks, I'll tell you about it."

"Good enough."

"We'll be approaching the outer limit of your destroyer screen in about three zero minutes."

"Roger that," Bozamato said. "I'll alert my destroyer captains."

"Tell them I'll be on a two two seven degree heading."

Bozamato repeated the *Turtle*'s heading.

"As soon as sonar contact is made, I'll surface," Boxer said. "I need some time on the surface to check the damage —"

"Say no more. If you need anything by way of repair crews, just let me know."

"Thanks," Boxer said. "I'll come alongside of the *Shiloh*."

"Roger that," Bozamato answered and added, "I'll be looking for you, Jack."

Smiling, Boxer put the phone down. "Even though the admiral was two years ahead of me at the academy, we became good friends. Do you know him?"

Cowly shook his head.

"He's a short, slightly built man with a well-trimmed beard and very wide eyes."

"I may have seen him several times, but I never had the pleasure of meeting him."

"He has a dry sense of humor and —"

The MO keyed Boxer. "Skipper, Captain Bush requests permission to go to the bridge."

"Tell him I'm coming to see him," Boxer said.

"Aye, aye, Skipper."

Boxer turned to Cowly. "You take the CONN. As soon as we make sonar contact with one of Shield's destroyers, ID it; then radio its skipper that we're going to surface."

"Do you want me to key you?"

Boxer shook his head. "You take us up," he said, leaving the swivel chair in front of the COMCOMP. "As soon as you're on the surface, contact the *Shiloh* and bring us alongside of her."

"Aye, aye, Skipper," Cowly answered, taking his position at the COMCOMP.

Boxer left the bridge and went straight to the sick bay where the doctor was waiting for him.

"How is Captain Bush?" Boxer asked.

"As normal as we are," the doctor answered.

Boxer nodded. "I want to speak to him alone."

"You'll have to use my office," the doctor said. "There are two men from the assault team in the sick bay with the captain."

"How are they doing?"

"One has metal fragments in his right leg and the other is suffering from shock and exhaustion."

"I'll see if I can have them transferred to the *Shiloh* and then flown back to the States from Italy."

"That would be the best thing for them," the doc said; then gesturing toward the sick bay, he said, "He's in uniform and sitting alongside his bed."

Boxer entered the sick bay.

Bush stood up. "I —"

Boxer held up his hand and said, "I'll be with you in a few moments, Captain. I want to speak to these men first." And he stopped between the two beds.

Both men managed to smile at him.

"I'm going to try and arrange to have you flown home," Boxer said, realizing that, though both were in their early twenties, they looked ten years older.

"Thanks, Skipper," one of them answered.

Boxer smiled and turned to Bush. "Captain, I'd appreciate it if you joined me."

"Aye, aye, Skipper," Bush said and left his bedside.

"In here," Boxer said, directing Bush into the doctor's office.

Bush waited until Boxer had closed the door before, and then he said, "I want to return to duty."

"Sit down," Boxer said.

"I'd rather stand."

Boxer sat down on the chair in front of the desk and took the time to fill and light his pipe. "I guess there's no other way, but to give it to you straight. I can't permit you to return to duty. That's for your own good and more importantly, for the good of crew."

Bush flushed.

"Why don't you sit down," Boxer suggested, softening the tone of his voice.

Bush nodded and sat in the chair alongside the desk.

"Have you any recollection of what happened?" Boxer asked.

"Not really."

Boxer puffed on his pipe.

"Bits and pieces," Bush told him after a long pause. "I seem to remember being in your quarters. Commander Lowe was there and then I think the doc came."

"Something like that happened," Boxer said, aware of the expression of helplessness on the man's face.

Bush shook his head. "All I want to do is go back to duty," he said.

"I'm sorry. I can't permit that."

"'Can't,' or 'won't,' Captain?"

Boxer put his pipe down. "Steven," he said, using Bush's given name, "I can't risk it. I —"

He was interrupted by the sound of the klaxon. Then Cowly's voice came over the MC. "Now hear this... Now hear this... This is Commander Cowly speaking... stand by to surface... Stand by to surface."

"I should be at the COMCOMP," Bush said angrily.

Boxer took a deep breath and slowly exhaled. He realized that Bush was in pain and there was nothing he could say or do to either ease or eliminate it. "Steve —"

"I'm as normal as you —"

"Surface... Surface... Surface," Cowly announced over the MC.

"Yes," Boxer said. "Now you're normal. But what would happen if you're at the COMCOMP and —"

"It won't happen. I know it won't."

Suddenly the *Turtle* seemed to push forward. Boxer frowned. The next instant the klaxon sounded three times.

Cowly's voice came over the MC. "Crash-dive... Crash-dive... Crash-dive!"

Boxer was on his feet and racing out of the MO's office.

"I'm coming with you," Bush shouted after him.

The *Turtle* was down at the bow and sinking fast.

Boxer reached the bridge and rushed to the COMCOMP. "What the hell —"

Cowly pointed to the sonar scope.

A target was coming straight at them.

"Holy Christ!" Boxer exclaimed. "She's less than five zero yards from us."

Suddenly there was a loud bang.

Several red lights on the COMCOMP went on.

Boxer ran SYSCHECK. All systems were green.

"Target one zero yards," the SO reported.

"Roger that," Boxer answered.

The DCO keyed Boxer. "Aft torpedo room flooding."

"The damn seal gave way!' Boxer exclaimed.

"Recommend all personnel be evacuated from the aft torpedo room," the DCO said.

"Roger that," Boxer answered and, switching on the MC, he said, "All personnel, evacuate the aft torpedo room... Repeat, evacuate the aft torpedo room... Section chief report."

The section chief reported. "All personnel clear."

Boxer electronically sealed off the aft torpedo room.

"Target passing overhead," the SO said.

The throb of the destroyer's screws filled the *Turtle*.

Boxer looked up and with his hand wiped the sweat from his face. Then he checked the depth gauge. They were fifty feet down. He keyed the DO. "Stand by to bring her level."

"Standing by," the DO answered.

The DCO keyed Boxer. "Skipper, we're taking a lot of water... More than the pumps can handle."

"Roger that," Boxer answered. He keyed the COMMO. "Get me Admiral Bozamato."

"Aye, aye, Skipper," the COMMO answered.

Boxer checked the ELI. The *Turtle* was going down at the stern. He keyed the DO. "Blow all ballast... Diving planes up one five degrees."

"Blowing all ballast... Diving planes at one five degrees."

The hiss of escaping air rushed through the *Turtle*.

The COMMO keyed Boxer. "The admiral is on, Skipper."

"Admiral," Boxer said, forcing the tone of his voice to remain calm, "we have an emergency... We are taking water."

"Say that again," Bozamato told him.

Boxer repeated the message; then added, "Have your group stand by... Have your group stand by... I'll radio condition."

"Roger that," Bozamato said.

The DO keyed Boxer. "We're still going down, Skipper."

"Flood all ballast tanks... Level diving planes."

"All ballast tanks flooding... Diving planes going to null."

"Roger that," Boxer said. Then he turned to Cowly. "Where's the bottom?" he asked.

Cowly turned on the fathometer. "Four hundred feet."

"Stand by at the UWIS and let me know what kind of landing we're going to make."

"Aye, aye," Cowly answered.

Boxer keyed the DCO. "We're going down to eight zero zero feet... Can the aft torpedo room bulkhead take that pressure?"

"For a while... Probably."

Boxer switched on the MC. "Now hear this... All hands, now hear this... We have an emergency... The *Turtle* will come to rest four hundred feet below the surface... We will attempt to make the necessary repairs." He put the mike down and checked the fathometer. They were one hundred feet off the bottom. He keyed the EO. "Stop all engines."

"Stopping all engines," the EO answered.

"Better take a look," Cowly said, pointing to the UWIS.

Boxer switched the image to the secondary scope. "Goddamn, it looks like every damn boulder in the world is down there." He switched on the MC. "All hands... All hands, brace yourselves. We're going to have a rough landing... All hands, brace yourselves... We're going to come down hard."

The DCO keyed Boxer. "Skipper, I suggest you pull everyone in toward the bridge and seal off the remainder of the stern and at least a third of the bow."

"Not enough time," Boxer answered, checking the UWIS. The *Turtle* was coming down fast. He switched on the MC. "All hands, brace yourselves... Brace yourselves!"

The *Turtle* crashed down an several boulders, bounced, and then rolled to the port side, grinding her metal plates against the rocks.

The lights dimmed and then brightened to their full strength.

Boxer was thrown against the COMCOMP.

"Skipper," the DCO said, keying Boxer, "we have major structural damage on the port side... We're taking water in the bow."

"Roger that," Boxer answered. He switched on the MC. "All hands, move to the bridge... All hands, to the bridge." He turned to Cowly. "Get a head count. As soon as everyone is here, we'll seal off the bow."

"Aye, aye, Skipper," Cowly answered.

Boxer keyed the COMMO. "Send a Mayday to the *Shiloh*... Give her our position... Tell her we're down four zero zero feet... Have her stand on station... Tell her to contact us as soon as she's on station."

"Roger that," the COMMO answered.

Boxer ran a SYSCHECK. The reactor system was green. The air system was green. But the fresh-water system and the hydraulic system were dangerously close to being red.

"Everyone present and accounted for," Cowly reported.

Boxer set several switches. An outline drawing of the *Turtle* filled one of the viewing screens. "We're almost red on the hydraulic system," he explained. "Better send a few men forward to seal off the bow. Close all bulkhead doors from number one to number five. That will leave the mess area still usable."

"Aye, aye, Skipper," Cowly answered.

Boxer glanced over his shoulder. The entire crew was there and they were looking at him. He knew they were waiting for an explanation. He took several deep breaths, stood up, and turned toward them. "Can everyone hear me? Good. We're not in a very good situation," he said. "We've taken on too much water to get to the surface."

A low, anxious murmur passed through the crew.

"But every one of us will reach the surface. We'll just get wet doing it."

"You mean you're going to abandon ship!" Bush exclaimed.

Boxer nodded. "That's exactly what we're going to do. She might be able to be salvaged. That's something I'll know after a while. But that kind of salvage operation will take days, maybe weeks, and we don't have that kind of time."

The COMMO keyed Boxer. "Message sent, Skipper... Admiral Bozamato has ordered the *Shiloh* on station and is standing by for your directions."

"Roger that," Boxer answered. Then turning his attention back to Bush, he said, "Don't worry, Captain. We will abandon the *Turtle* only if there is no other choice."

"I'm certainly glad to hear that," Bush answered stiffly.

Boxer was afraid that Bush was going to give him trouble, when he already had more than he could probably handle. "Those of you who are not needed on the bridge go the mess area. Commander Lowe, Lieutenant De Vargas, and the DCO, please remain on the bridge."

"Captain," Bush said, "I would —"

"I'm sorry. You'll have to leave the bridge," Boxer said.

"Is that a direct order?"

Boxer hesitated, then said, "It's a request, Steve."

Bush nodded, turned, and walked away.

Boxer breathed a quiet sigh of relief.

"Skipper," De Vargas said, "I could get a couple of men out and take a look at the damage."

"Okay. Use men from the DC station. I don't want your —" He felt the *Turtle* begin to roll to the port side.

"We're slipping!" Cynthia exclaimed.

The hull of the *Turtle* ground along the side of the boulders.

"Grab onto something!" Boxer shouted. He switched on the MC. "All hands to the starboard side... All hands to the starboard side."

"Son of a bitch, she's going over!" De Vargas swore.

The lights went out.

Boxer fumbled for the emergency light switch and pushed it. The lights came back on again, but not nearly as strong as they had been before.

"We're on the bottom," Cowly said, looking at the UWIS.

"We're on our goddamn port side," Boxer answered. "We're over about three five degrees." He turned to the DCO. "Get us on even keel."

"I'll have to go back to the DC center."

Boxer shook his head. "Try it from the COMCOMP."

The DCO motioned to Cynthia and the two of them stepped up to the COMCOMP.

"Skipper," said the DCO, "we're losing structural integrity in the forward torpedo room."

Boxer acknowledged the report with a nod.

The COMMO keyed Boxer. "Admiral Stark is on the radio," he said.

Boxer switched on the speaker. "Captain Boxer here," he said.

"What the devil is happening?" Stark asked.

"We're down," Boxer answered.

"How bad?"

"Four five eight feet of water and over three five degrees on our port side... The aft torpedo room is completely flooded and we're taking water in the forward torpedo room."

"Any casualties?"

"Only in the raid," Boxer answered.

"Can you bring her up?"

"Can't answer... Right now the DCO is trying to put her on an even keel."

"Roger that," Stark answered.

Boxer switched the radio off and, leaning back into his chair for a moment, he closed his eyes — Stark expected him to bring the *Turtle* home. Anything less, though he would never say so, would be unacceptable — Boxer opened his eyes and pursed his lips — Maybe there was a way. Maybe he wasn't thinking of all the angles. Maybe he was thinking of how to save the lives of his crew rather than gambling them on a salvage operation that might fail...

"Skipper," Cynthia said, "we'll have to pump water out of the port-side ballast tanks and hope we can balance it with the starboard side."

"Suppose we blow all ballast?" Boxer answered.

"We'd rise — but not enough."

"Enough to force-pump the water out of the forward torpedo room?"

Cynthia nodded.

"The trouble is in the aft torpedo room," the DCO said. "We still have that ruptured pressure seal to worry about... That's where the problem began."

Boxer nodded. "We'll jettison everything we can... All ammo, missiles, torpedoes... That should gain us some feet."

"It won't be enough to overcome the weight —"

"Let's find out just how close to the surface we can get," Boxer told him.

"Skipper," Cynthia said, "we're going to lose the protection of the plastic shield."

"It's a risk we're going to have to take," Boxer answered. He switched on the MC. "Now hear this... All hands, now hear this... We're going to make an attempt to save this boat... All hands, return to your duty stations... All hands, return to your duty stations."

Bush came on the bridge, followed by the MO.

"I told him to return to the sick bay," the MO complained.

The SO keyed Boxer. "Have the *Shiloh* and escorts on the scope."

"Roger that," Boxer said.

The COMMO keyed Boxer. "Admiral Bozamato reports the *Shiloh* coming on station."

"Patch him in," Boxer said.

"Aye, aye, Skipper," the COMMO answered.

"Jack, you should be hearing us any moment," Bozamato said.

"Admiral, we're going to try and make it to the surface... How's the weather up there?"

"Still foggy as hell."

"Have your escort and support ships either dead in the water, or at least twenty-five-thousand yards away from the *Shiloh*."

"Roger that... Good luck."

Boxer switched off the radio phone and turned to Bush. "Either you return to sick bay on your own, or I'll have you taken there under guard."

Bush glared at him.

"The choice is yours," Boxer said.

Bush did an about face and walked stiffly away.

"Watch him," Boxer said. Then he keyed the DO. "Blow all ballast."

"Aye, aye, Skipper."

The hiss of air filled the *Turtle*.

Boxer felt the boat move. His eyes went to the roll indicator. The needle was fluttering, then moved ten degrees toward null. It hung there for a few moments and jumped another twelve degrees. He checked the overhead depth gauge. The *Turtle* was up fifty feet and still rising.

Boxer keyed the EO. "Stand by to deliver full power."

"Standing by to deliver full power," the EO answered.

The DCO keyed Boxer. "Down one five degrees at the stern, Skipper."

"Roger that," Boxer said; then he switched on the MC. "Forward torpedo room, fire all torpedoes... Set for one zero feet... Range five zero zero yards... Do not arm."

Boxer watched the COMCOMP. The red firing lights began to flash; then they turned to green. "The first salvo is away," Boxer announced.

"Bow up zero four degrees," Cowly reported.

Boxer keyed the DCO. "Vent all drinking water."

The DCO hesitated.

"Vent all drinking water," Boxer said sharply.

"Aye, aye, Skipper," the DCO answered.

"Coming to even keel," Cowly said.

Boxer's eyes flicked toward the roll indicator. Satisfied, he looked at the EDI. The *Turtle* had gained a total of one hundred and fifty feet and was still rising.

The red firing lights lit up again; then turned green.

"Bow up zero four degrees," Cowly said.

Boxer keyed the missile officer. "Fire at will."

"Skipper, none of the birds will break the surface."

"Fire!" Boxer ordered.

The firing sequence began.

Suddenly the throb of the *Shiloh*'s propellers passed over, then through, the *Turtle*.

"Gained two five feet," Cowly reported.

Boxer check the overhead depth gauge and compared it to the readings on the DDRO. They were exactly the same: the *Turtle* was still two hundred feet below the surface. He keyed the TO. "Prepare torpedo tubes to jettison all ammo."

"Aye, aye, Skipper," the TO said.

Boxer turned to Cowly. "We're not going to make it to the surface unless we can vent the aft torpedo room of some, if not all, of the water."

"There is a way," Cowly said. "It's a long shot but it might work."

"I'm listening."

"We get divers from the *Shiloh* to weld the propeller shaft to the hull. Then they make four openings — two on each side of the hull. Into two of the openings they attach high-pressure air hoses. That should enable us to vent at least half the water in there and bring us up very close to the surface, where the rest of the water can be pumped out."

Boxer nodded appreciatively. "It's worth a try, but I want all hands on the surface. I don't want to risk anyone, if it should fail."

"The *Turtle* will have to be towed back to Norfolk," Cowly said.

"That's a hell of a lot better than not coming back at all."

The TO keyed Boxer. "All tubes loaded and ready," he reported.

"How long will it take to get rid of all our ammo?" Boxer asked.

"Not more than one zero minutes."

"Fire at will," Boxer said.

"Roger that," the TO answered.

Boxer faced Cowly. "Let's see where we wind up before I call the admiral."

The DCO keyed Boxer. "We're still taking water in the bow section."

"Can the pumps handle it?"

"Just about."

"Roger that," Boxer answered, watching the torpedo firing lights go from red to green.

The COMMO keyed Boxer. "Admiral Stark is on the radio phone."

"Tell him I'll get back to him as soon as I can," Boxer said.

"Aye, aye, Skipper," the COMMO responded.

Boxer watched the depth gauge. With each firing, the *Turtle* gained five feet.

The TO keyed Boxer. "All ammo jettisoned," he reported.

"Roger that," Boxer said and keyed the COMMO. "Connect me to Admiral Bozamato."

"Aye, aye, Skipper."

Boxer checked the depth gauge against the DDRO. They matched. The *Turtle* was one hundred feet down.

"I'm on," Bozamato said.

"Admiral, my EXO came up with a plan that might just save the *Turtle*."

"Let's have it."

Boxer explained Cowly's plan.

"It sounds like it's the only game in town," Bozamato said.

"My crew will start to surface within one zero minutes," Boxer told Bozamato. "Your divers should be ready to come down immediately."

"Roger that," Bozamato said.

"How's the fog up there?"

"Still thick."

"The first man up will fire flares at zero two minute intervals," Boxer said.

"I'll have boats over the side ready to pick them up."

"Admiral, I'm remaining with the *Turtle* until she's brought to the surface," Boxer said.

"Are you certain that's necessary?"

"Yes."

"Good luck, Jack."

"Thanks, Phil… Let's hope I don't have to depend on luck."

"Roger that," Bozamato said.

Boxer switched on the MC. "All hands, now hear this… All hands… Now hear this… We are going to attempt to save the *Turtle*, but to ensure everyone's safety, the *Turtle* must be abandoned… All hands, stand by to abandon ship… Stand by to abandon ship… Each section will exit through the outer bridge hatch... Mr. Cowly will be in command... First section to leave will be engineering... Second section will be all torpedo personnel, forward and aft... Third section will be dive control... CIC will follow... All other personnel will abandon ship in an orderly manner... Mr. Cowly will be the last officer to leave... The first man on the surface will fire flares at zero two minute intervals... You will be picked up by boats from the *Shiloh*... Good luck, and I'll see you aboard the *Shiloh*." Boxer switched off the mike and turned to Cowly. "Start getting the men out in zero seven minutes."

"Skipper —"

"Better get to your station in the outer bridge chamber," Boxer said.

Cowly nodded.

"Good luck," Boxer said.

"Good luck to you, Skipper," Cowly answered.

The COMMO keyed Boxer. "Skipper, the *Shiloh* reports four divers are on their way down."

"Roger that," Boxer replied.

"Skipper —" Cynthia began.

"Commander Lowe, you will accompany Mr. Cowly to the outer bridge hatch immediately," Boxer said tersely; then he added a moment later, in a softer tone, "You'll be all right."

"Will you?"

Boxer nodded.

"Captain," Bush shouted, coming up to the bridge, "I absolutely refuse to abandon ship!"

"I'm sorry, Skipper," the MO said, from behind Bush, "I tried to stop him, but he pushed past me."

"Captain," Boxer said calmly, "I intended to ask you to stay with me."

"What?"

"I will certainly need your assistance," Boxer continued in a matter-of-fact tone, "and since you're the only officer equal in rank to myself, I thought I would ask you to remain."

"You were going to do that?"

"Yes. But first I want you to know that we will probably go down with the *Turtle*."

"Go down?"

"There is little hope that she can be raised. What I told the crew was for their benefit. But what I tell you, I tell you because of your rank."

Bush looked confused; then he said, "In that case I think it would be better if I surfaced and took command of the crew aboard the *Shiloh*."

"If that's what you think is best, then I have no choice but to agree with you," Boxer said, offering his hand.

Bush shook it, stepped back, saluted, and, turning around, he left the bridge.

"Doc, please wait a few moments," Boxer requested and when Bush was out of earshot, he said, "Report his condition to Admiral Bozamato and then have him taken down to the sick bay area and handed over to the ship's MO."

"I'll be glad to get him off my hands," the MO said.

"Will the Lieutenant's men be able to make it?" Boxer asked.

"Yes. It won't be easy, but they should be able to do it."

"See you topside," Boxer said.

"Good luck, Skipper," the MO answered.

The COMMO keyed Boxer. "The divers are in position on the stern, Skipper."

"Roger that," Boxer said.

"I'll set up the radio so you can keep in contact with the divers and the *Shiloh* from the COMCOMP," the COMMO told him.

"Thanks," Boxer said. He fished out his pipe, filled, and lit it. Ordinarily he never smoked while he had the CONN. But this was far from an ordinary situation. Even though he knew that part of the crew was still aboard, the boat was strangely silent already.

One of the divers keyed him. "Captain, beginning to weld the shaft to the hull plates."

"Roger that," Boxer said. He closed his eyes and leaned back into the swivel chair. He was very tired and this wait would further exhaust him. He promised himself a long vacation with Trish when he returned to the States. "A long, wonderful vacation," he said aloud, "where there's sun and —"

Bozamato keyed him and said, "Spotted the first flares… The boats are beginning to pick up your crew."

Boxer opened his eyes. "Let me know if you have all of them… Mr. Cowly has the head count."

"Roger that," Bozamato answered.

Boxer checked the COMCOMP. The *Turtle*, like the *Shark*, would be held automatically in neutral buoyancy. She was there now, one hundred feet below the surface. She would not move up or down and, if she did because of the movement of a current or a change in water temperature, she would automatically be brought back to one hundred feet.

He ran a SYSCHECK. All systems were green, with the exception of the hydraulic and the fresh water. Luckily neither were needed for the salvage operation.

Boxer puffed on his pipe. His thoughts strayed to Trish and the possibility of their making some sort of a life together. Their last argument was still fresh in his mind. She was certainly used to having her own way and, he had to admit, on a different level so was he. But the real differences between them lay in that he understood the meaning of duty and she didn't; he had strong loyalties and hers were —

"Skipper, about now I could use a drink."

Even before he turned, Boxer recognized De Vargas's voice. "What the hell are you doing here?"

"The truth?"

"The truth," Boxer said.

"I couldn't have made it to the top."

Boxer cocked his head to the right. "Why?"

"A couple of broken ribs."

"Does the doc know?"

De Vargas shook his head. "Time enough for that when we get to the surface." Then he smiled. "Besides, I knew you wouldn't mind the company."

"You're a pain in the ass," Boxer said.

De Vargas shrugged.

Cowly keyed Boxer. "Skipper, the Lieutenant hasn't surfaced."

"He's here," Boxer said.

"Ten four," Cowly answered.

"Might as well make yourself comfortable," Boxer said, "it will be a while before anything happens."

De Vargas pulled a chair over and sat down. "I feel as if I'm a hundred and fifty years old," he said.

Boxer nodded sympathetically. "After a couple of weeks' rest with Nicole and you'll be better than new."

"Rest with Nicole, you've gotta be joking!"

"Bragging or complaining?"

"Just telling it like it is," De Vargas said with a grin. "What about you and —"

Bozamato keyed Boxer. "Jack, Captain Bush went bananas. He had to be restrained."

"Roger that," Boxer answered.

"The divers have finished the welding," Bozamato said. "They're going to punch holes in the hull and put in the high-pressure air hoses... Engineering says we have to deliver two five percent more pressure than your ambient pressure."

"Standing by," Boxer said.

"How long do you think it will take before we start to move toward the surface?" De Vargas asked.

"Not too long, I hope."

The chief of the diver team keyed Boxer. "Captain, we've burned two holes on the starboard side of the aft torpedo room and two on the port... The HP air hoses are coming down... We should begin to deliver air in about one five minutes."

"Roger that," Boxer answered, facing De Vargas.

"Too bad we don't have a deck of cards —"

"What's wrong?" Boxer asked.

De Vargas pointed to the COMCOMP.

Boxer turned. A bank of lights were blinking red. "The forward pumps are failing."

"What?"

Boxer keyed the *Shiloh*. "Abandoning ship... Mayday... Mayday... Abandoning ship."

"Roger that," Bozamato answered.

"Com'on," Boxer said, throwing the necessary switches to close down the reactor, "let's get the hell out of here."

"Skipper, I can't —"

Boxer grabbed hold of De Vargas's arm. "Move."

The two of them left the bridge and headed up the steps leading to the outer bridge hatch.

Suddenly the *Turtle* pitched forward.

"The hull has caved in at the bow," Boxer said. "Get your mask on."

De Vargas nodded.

"Now help me push the flood valve open," Boxer said.

"Jammed," De Vargas exclaimed.

"Better not be, or we're dead," Boxer said. "Together... Now!"

The valve stick moved and water began to pour into the escape hatch.

Boxer pointed up to the overhead hatch lock. In a few moments he had it open and motioned to De Vargas to leave the *Turtle*. Suddenly he realized that the man had lost his nerve. He motioned to him again and this time, he reached down and pulled him up toward the opening — De Vargas was out and he followed.

Boxer glanced down at the *Turtle*: it was dropping toward the bottom. And then out of the corner of his eye he saw De Vargas going down too. He arched down and, with a half-a-dozen powerful strokes, he was close enough to be able to grab him in a headlock and start the long hard climb toward the surface...

Minutes later, Boxer surfaced in the bright white circle of floodlights and the cheers of the men on the *Shiloh*.

"Lieutenant, we made it," Boxer gasped. "We made it."

De Vargas didn't answer.

"Lieutenant —" Boxer clutched De Vargas to him, but he was dead.

CHAPTER 4

A few hours after being rescued, the *Turtle*'s entire crew was flown to the da Vinci airport in Rome where they boarded a commercial jet for the flight back to the States.

Boxer chose a window seat, on the port side, just forward off the wing. No one sat next to him. De Vargas's death affected him deeply. An autopsy had shown De Vargas had bled to death internally. The MO had said that the physical effort required to get out of the *Turtle* probably caused the rib to pierce the lung.

Boxer pursed his lips. De Vargas's body was being flown back with them. He and the members of the crew would be at the funeral two days after the plane landed in New York.

Boxer turned his thoughts toward Trish. He had spoken to her by radiophone from the *Shiloh* and had wanted to ask her to meet him in New York. But he had sensed his call had disturbed her and had said instead that he'd be returning to Washington in a few days. The conversation had left him completely unsatisfied.

The plane eased away from the terminal, rolled out onto the runway, and joined a long line of aircraft waiting to take off.

"Ladies and gentlemen," the flight attendant announced, "on behalf of Signet Airlines, welcome aboard Flight Forty-four from Rome to New York. Captain Standish says we should be on our way in about ten minutes. Our estimated flying time will be eight hours and fifteen minutes. The temperature in New York is thirty degrees and it is snowing lightly. Thank you."

Boxer closed his eyes and leaned back. He hoped to sleep most of the flight. He knew that the next few days would be emotionally draining. He had never met anyone from De Vargas's family and now —

"Excuse me," a woman said, "but aren't you —?"

Boxer opened his eyes and found himself looking up at Francine Wheeler, the lawyer he'd met in Admiral Stark's office a few weeks before.

"May I sit down?" she asked.

"Please," Boxer responded, though he would have preferred to be alone.

"I was hoping to hear from you," she said, settling next to him. "The will has been probated and I have some papers for you to sign."

"I'm sorry. I really meant to call, but I did get to pay a visit to the Spadaro boy. He looks a lot like Rugger. He thinks he's a tough piece of work."

"Never met him," she said.

"I really would have called," Boxer explained, somehow feeling that more of an explanation was needed. "But I have been out of the country for the past couple of weeks."

"And there is the matter of that one painting, I mentioned to you. I'd like to have that settled too."

Boxer looked at her. She was a redhead. Even her eyebrows were the color of burnished copper. She had green eyes and was a half a head shorter than himself. She wore a light-green pants suit and a dark-green scarf around her neck. He realized she was a very attractive woman. Perhaps even beautiful.

"Is there any reason why you're staring at me?" she asked.

"Sorry. I didn't mean to," Boxer said.

Then she looked hard at him. "Is anything wrong?" she asked. "You look —"

Boxer held up his hand. "I'm just very tired."

"Skipper," Cowly said, suddenly coming up to the seat, "some of the men asked —" As soon as he saw that someone was sitting next to Boxer he stopped.

"Miss Wheeler, my EXO, Mr. Cowly," Boxer said.

Cowly and Wheeler shook hands.

"Miss Wheeler was Captain Rugger's lawyer," Boxer explained. Then he asked, "What's up?"

Cowly glanced at Wheeler; then looking back at Boxer, he said, "It can wait."

Boxer nodded.

"Nice to meet you, Miss Wheeler," Cowly said and returned to his seat.

Francine waited until Cowly was gone, before she said, "He didn't want to talk in front of me, did he?"

Boxer shrugged. "Probably not. But don't worry; I'll be told whatever it was that he wanted to tell me."

"Would you prefer it if I moved?" she asked.

"No," he said, shaking his head. "Actually, I'm glad you've sat down next to me. I was becoming too morose. Besides, I like the smell of your perfume. What is it?"

"I don't know what it is. I have it made for me."

"Now that's a first. I don't think I've ever known a woman who had her perfume made especially for her."

"Ah, Captain, I just don't think you know the right kind of woman," Wheeler answered with a smile.

"That's possible," Boxer answered. "That's entirely possible."

The conversation between the two of them lapsed.

The pilot announced that they were crossing the coast of southern France.

Boxer looked out of the window. He could see the azure water, white sand beaches, and the hills beyond them. He turned to Wheeler and asked, "Would you like to take a look?"

"I've been to the Riviera with my ex-husband," she said. "I didn't care for it then and I have no desire to look down on it from thirty-five-thousand feet."

Boxer said nothing and continued to look out of the window until he could no longer see the beach without straining. Then he rested against the back of the seat and closed his eyes.

"Captain," Wheeler asked softly, "are you all right?"

Boxer opened his eyes and seeing the look of concern on her face, he said, "I'm not all right. I'm exhausted. I shouldn't be telling you any of this, but maybe I'll feel better if I do."

"Whatever you tell me will remain with me," she answered.

He nodded. "If I didn't think it would, I would not have mentioned anything." He paused. "My entire crew is aboard."

"I saw all those men when I came on," she said. "I thought they were members of some team. Most of them are so young."

Boxer took a deep breath and, slowly exhaling, he turned his face toward the window. "The rest of them never made it."

"I don't think I understand," she said in a tremulous voice.

He looked at her and said, "They're dead." Then he looked down at the floor.

"How?"

Boxer shook his head. "Can't tell you that," he said in a choked voice. "I've already breached security."

"Many?"

"Many," he answered and after a few moments he felt her hand on his. He looked at her.

"I'm so sorry," she said.

Boxer's vision blurred and he faced the window again.

"Captain, it's no shame to weep."

He cleared his throat. "I know that." And looking at her he said, "Thanks, Miss Wheeler."

"Francine."

"Thanks, Francine," Boxer said.

"Captain —"

"Jack."

She nodded. "I wouldn't be much of a person if I couldn't at least listen to another person in distress. I only wish I could do something more."

"No need to worry. After I get some sleep, I'll be fine."

"Why don't you close your eyes and try to sleep now," Francine suggested.

"I don't think it will work."

"Try for me," she said, squeezing his hand.

"It's not going to —"

"Please."

Boxer nodded, settled back into the seat, and, with a deep sigh, he closed his eyes. The last thing he was aware of was the softness of her hand.

Boxer woke slowly, with the scent of perfume in his nostrils and a growing awareness that he was resting on someone's shoulder. He opened his eyes and found himself looking down at the slow rise and fall of a woman's breast. Then he realized her head was resting against his own. He caught a glimpse of her red hair and remembered who she was.

Boxer looked toward the window. Below was the ocean. He was about to look at his watch without disturbing her. He had slept about an hour.

Suddenly a stewardess came up to him. "I didn't want to wake you, sir, but we're almost finished serving lunch. Would you and your companion want —"

Francine lifted her head.

"I was just asking if you wanted lunch?" the stewardess said. Then suddenly she stepped back and with a broad smile, she asked, "Aren't you Captain Boxer?"

"In the flesh," Boxer answered.

"I was the other stew on board the plane that you —" She looked at Francine. "He shot it out with a couple of hijackers. Didn't he tell you about it?"

"Yes, I think I will have lunch," Boxer said, hoping to change the subject. "What are the choices?"

Still speaking to Francine, the stewardess said, "Every one of the crew on that flight has made him our personal hero. And I hate to tell you what the stews say about him."

"Oh, please tell me," Francine said.

"There really isn't any need to tell her," Boxer said, feeling the color in his cheeks.

"Listen, Captain," the stewardess said, "more than most women, stews know a real man when they see one. And you're one."

"What do the stews say about him?" Francine asked, her green eyes twinkling with laughter.

"Me included?"

"Of course you included."

The stewardess looked at Boxer. "None of us would mind having your shoes parked under her bed."

Boxer began to cough.

"Well, now," Francine said in mock seriousness, "you've got quite an invitation, Captain!"

Boxer found his voice. "I'm flattered —"

"Flattered!" Francine laughed. "That's hardly a strong-enough emotion. You should be ecstatic. You should most certainly rise to the occasion." She turned toward the stewardess. "Just how many stews were aboard that plane?"

"Six.'

"Why, Captain, that certainly is a challenge!" Francine exclaimed.

"Thank them. And thank you," Boxer said and, putting his arm around Francine's shoulders, he added, "My shoes are under her bed. But if —"

"What did you just say?" Francine asked, trying to wiggle free.

Boxer held her fast. "If there should be any change," he said, "I'll certainly try to find you."

"Your shoes aren't —"

"Lunch," Boxer said. "What are the choices?"

"Chicken Kiev, lamb chops á la Grec, and filet of sole stuffed with crabmeat," the stewardess said.

"The chicken Kiev sounds fine," Boxer said. "And what would you like?" he asked, looking at Francine.

"The same."

"Would you care for a drink?"

Francine shook her head. "I'm not a drinker. I have one and I go off."

"One vodka on the rocks," Boxer told the stewardess.

The stewardess smiled at them and went back to the galley.

"That was a low blow," Francine said. "Now she thinks there's something between us."

"There is. We have an estate to settle and a painting to discuss," Boxer said, withdrawing his arm.

Francine's cheeks reddened.

"You're blushing," Boxer teased.

"No, I'm not!"

Boxer accepted the denial without comment.

"It was still a low blow," Francine said.

"And what about your comment about rising to the occasion."

"That was witty. You'd certainly have to admit that."

"But at my expense," Boxer said.

"Only a little —"

He took hold of her face between his hands and kissed her on the lips.

"Why did you do that?" she asked.

"To stop you from talking," Boxer answered.

She nodded and, after a few moments of silence, she said. "How was your sleep?"

"Good. And yours?"

"Nice."

"Did you really do what she said you did?"

"I just happened to be there," he answered. "Anyone could have done the same thing."

The stewardess returned with the vodka.

"To you and your five friends," Boxer toasted, looking up at the stewardess before he drank.

"You made her day," Francine said.

"And you made mine," Boxer said, lifting the plastic cup toward Francine. "Thank you."

She blushed. "I'm glad I did."

Boxer took hold of her hand and squeezed it. "I hope the guy whose shoes are under your bed knows he's got a very special lady."

"He didn't. That's why his shoes aren't there anymore."

"He's a fool," Boxer said.

"No," she countered in a whisper, "I was for letting him put them there in the first place."

"I've made a few mistakes myself," he said, kissing the back of her hand.

She turned away from him.

He put his hand under her chin and eased her face toward him. "No tears," he said gently. "Please, don't cry." And with his handkerchief, he brushed away the tears.

"I'm sorry," she said. "I don't have a right to burden you with my personal problems. It's just that —"

Boxer put his finger across her lips. "Don't say any more. It's not a matter of you having the right or not. You have the right to tell me anything you want. I just don't want you to —" He paused to search for the right words. "You even have the right to weep," he continued, "if that's what you want to do. But—"

"I'm all right now," she said.

"Sure?"

"Sure," she answered with a nod. "I must look a mess. If you'll excuse me, I'd like to go and fix myself up."

"You look fine to me."

"That's because you have tears in your eyes too," she said. "Only yours don't smudge your mascara or eyeshadow."

Boxer nodded. "Are you sure you don't want something to drink?"

"Positive," she said, unbuckling the seat belt and standing.

Boxer looked up at her and saw she was a far more beautiful woman than he previously had realized.

"Is anything wrong?" she asked.

Boxer shook his head. He would have liked to stand up and stroke her face, but he did know he didn't have the right.

"I'll be back in time for lunch," she told him with a smile.

"Good. I'll wait," Boxer said and he looked out of the window. Far below the shadow of the plane skimmed along the surface of the sunlit ocean and he realized that his shadow was never any great distance from him either. To see it, all he had to do was close his eyes and it would be in front of him with all its horrors, with all its fears. But he also knew that, as long as he was strong enough to keep it behind him, he could still command.

"Skipper?"

Boxer turned and looked up at Cowly.

"Was the De Vargas family notified?" Cowly asked.

"Kinkade said it would be done," Boxer answered.

"Will they be at the airport?"

"I hope not."

"But what happens to the body?"

"It will be picked up by a funeral home," Boxer said. "I imagine the De Vargases will make the arrangements."

"What about Nicole?"

"I'll contact her. I'll have her flown up from Washington."

Cowly nodded; and then he asked, "Are all of us going to stay at the same hotel?"

"That would make it easier for everyone," Boxer answered, just as Francine returned.

Cowly stood up. "See you when we land," he said, moving aside to let Francine sit down.

"Keep the men together," Boxer said. "I don't want them wandering off to make telephone calls. They can do that when they reach the hotel. Remind them to maintain security."

"Aye, aye, Skipper," Cowly answered and retreated toward the rear of the aircraft.

Francine smiled at him. "That sounded very military," she said.

"It was," Boxer said.

"Ah, here comes the food!" Francine said, releasing the table top from the rear seat in front of her.

"I'm suddenly very hungry," Boxer commented.

"That's a good sign. When a man loses interest in food and sex it becomes serious."

"I guess my condition isn't serious. I still have a very healthy interest in the two activities."

"I'm glad," she said, "for the woman who has your shoes under her bed."

Boxer didn't answer. If he didn't have Trish, he'd try to get to know her better. There was much about her that appealed to him. Much that —

"A penny for your thoughts," Francine said.

"They're about you," he answered. "And they're not for sale."

Blushing, she said, "I'm glad they're not for sale."

"A matter of security," Boxer responded.

"I understand —"

The NO SMOKING and FASTEN YOUR SEAT BELT signs began to flash over the top of the forward bulkhead.

"Ladies and gentlemen," a voice said, "this is Captain Standish speaking. Please give your undivided attention. We have just been informed by our British controller that a bomb has been planted aboard the aircraft."

A ragged gasp of fear filled the aircraft.

"Though we cannot be sure that a bomb is aboard, we must take all the necessary precautions. We are going to descend to a very low altitude and are changing our course to be near a couple of ships in the event that we might be forced to ditch. Please remain calm and follow the instructions of the flight attendants. I will keep you informed of further developments."

"Oh, my God!" Francine exclaimed.

"Take it easy," Boxer said gently. "Just take it easy." Then he rang for the stewardess. "Better clear these trays away," he told her. "And tell Captain Standish that there are several demolition experts aboard, who can help locate and then defuse the bomb."

She nodded and left.

As soon as the trays were cleared, Boxer secured both table tops to the rear of the seats in front of him and Francine. Then he stood up and started to move in the aisle.

"Where are you going?" Francine asked.

"To my men," Boxer answered. "I'll be back."

"But what if the bomb explodes —"

"Come with me," Boxer said, reaching down and unbuckling her seat belt. "Come."

"Captain Boxer," the stewardess called, "please remain in your seat. Please give me the names of the demolition experts."

Boxer and Francine moved back into their seats and Boxer said, "William McGinn, Robert Morris, and Frank Giodano. Those three will be able to help."

She nodded and went to the rear of the aircraft, where the *Turtle*'s crew was seated.

"This is Captain Standish. We are turning to the starboard and we will descend to an altitude of five hundred feet."

Boxer looked toward the window. The tip of the wing began to drop and the plane tilted sharply to the right.

"My ears are stuffed," Francine complained.

"Swallow," Boxer said, watching the waves become more sharply defined. "We're going down fast." He looked for the two ships but couldn't see them.

"I can't believe this is happening," Francine said.

Captain Standish came on again. "We've been informed by our British controller that the bomb is electronically controlled and will be detonated if this aircraft is not landed in Tripoli."

"Holy Christ," Boxer exclaimed, "they want us."

"You mean the bomb —"

"Is on board because I and my crew are on board," Boxer said.

"But how could they explode the bomb from Tripoli?"

"There must be a plane trailing us," Boxer said. He looked out of the window. "We're almost on the deck."

"I don't understand."

"We're flying just above the water," Boxer explained.

"Captain Boxer," the stewardess said, "Captain Standish asks you to come to the cockpit."

Boxer unbuckled his safety belt, stood up, and said to Francine, "Nothing is going to happen yet. Just keep calm."

"I'll try," she answered in a tight voice.

Boxer stepped into the aisle and followed the stewardess.

She opened the cockpit door and said, "Captain Boxer is here."

The flight engineer looked up at him.

"Come in," Captain Standish said. "I have your chief on the radio. He wants to speak to you." He handed a headset and mike to Boxer. "You're hooked in," he told him.

"Kinkade or Admiral Stark?" Boxer asked.

"The two of us are on," Stark said in his gravelly voice. "What's your recommendation?"

"There are two hundred and fifty people aboard in addition to my crew. I can't give you a recommendation. Those bastards want me and my men."

"Do you think they're bluffing?" Kinkade asked.

"My guess," Boxer said, "is that there's one of their aircraft in our vicinity."

"Captain Standish, how close are you to Iceland?" Stark asked.

"About an hour's flying time," Standish answered.

"That's in the wrong direction," Boxer said. "If we change course now —"

The co-pilot touched Standish's arm. "Our British controller is on," he said.

Standish adjusted several dials. "The British controller is on. All of us will be able to hear him."

"Flight four four... This is flight controller X-ray Charley from Wickingham Station... We still have you on our screens... There's another aircraft at an azimuth of two five three degrees... Keeping a steady five zero miles from you."

"Ten four," Standish said; then to the others on the hookup, he said, "That must be our shadow."

"Can you ditch?" Kinkade asked.

"Yes," Standish answered. "But we might have some casualties..."

"How long would you have before the aircraft would sink?" Stark asked.

"Three... Maybe five minutes," Standish answered. "Less if they detonate the bomb."

"Jack," Stark said, "the President is patched into our hookup."

"Roger that, sir," Boxer answered.

"Captain Boxer," the President said, "will your men be able to assist in the rescue?"

"As much as possible," Boxer answered. "But that means most of them will have to be out of the plane first... Everyone else will have to wait and we won't have much time before the aircraft goes down."

"I understand that," the President replied.

"Mr. President," Boxer said, "the men they took alive they impaled... Some had their genitals cut off and stuffed into their mouths."

"Ditch," the President ordered. "Ditch... Admiral, can any of our fighter planes get that son of a bitch that's tailing them?"

"I've scrambled a wing from our base in Iceland and another from a base in England... We'll get him one way or another."

"I want that bastard shot down."

"Yes, Mr. President," Stark answered; then to Standish he said, "Take her down, Captain, and good luck."

"Ten four," Standish replied and, turning toward Boxer, he said, "In a few minutes we should pick up those two ships. They're standing by for further instructions."

"Have them go slow ahead with about two hundred yards between them. Have them lower all boats and rafts. I want everything that can float out. From the looks of it the sea is calm."

Standish nodded.

"I'll explain the situation over the PA," Boxer said. "My crew will know what they have to do."

"Tell me when," Standish said, "and I'll switch you to the PA system."

"Did you ever ditch before?" Boxer asked.

"Never."

"Is there a hatch on the roof?"

"Yes. But to get to it, the ceiling would have to be ripped out, and we don't have the time to do that."

"Patch me into the PA," Boxer said.

"You're in," Standish whispered.

"Ladies and gentlemen," Boxer said, in a calm voice, this is Captain Jack Boxer of the United States Navy... I and my crew are traveling back to the States with you." He took a deep breath and slowly exhaled. "We are going to land in the sea. I cannot tell you that there is no danger involved. But if all of us keep calm and follow instructions, the danger will be minimized... There are two ships standing by to take on survivors... Captain Standish and his flight crew will give you the necessary instructions to protect yourself when we come down... After that, my men will assist you to exit the aircraft... But in order to do this, they must be allowed to leave the aircraft before anyone else... You must put your trust and your lives in their hands... I wish all of you good luck." He turned and nodded to Standish.

"You're disconnected," Standish said.

Boxer uttered a deep sigh and handing the earphones and mike back to Standish he said, "Let's hope that bomb doesn't go off before we get clear of the aircraft. Those bastards must know we're not flying a normal course."

Standish didn't answer. He was sweating profusely. Boxer left the cockpit and started toward the rear of the plane.

"Jack?" Francine called and reached up toward him.

He stopped. "I want you to move to another seat. My men will see you out of the aircraft."

"What about you?" she questioned, still holding onto his hand.

He ignored her question. "Mr. Cowly will reseat you," he said. "Now I must go to my men." And gently separating her hand from his, he bent down and kissed her on the lips. "You'll be okay. I'll see you soon." Then he turned away and continued along the aisle.

Cowly was waiting for him. "I've already made the assignments, Skipper. Four men will go out of each of the escape doors. Four more men will handle the rubber rafts on each side of the aircraft. The remainder of the men will see that all of the civilian passengers clear the aircraft. There are four children aboard. They'll leave first and there are seven infants. They'll go out with their mothers. The infants and mothers will be placed in the rubber rafts. Everyone else goes into the rafts if there's room, or into the drink."

Boxer nodded approvingly. "Move Miss Wheeler to another seat and have Cynthia keep an eye on her."

"Will do, Skipper."

Boxer looked at his men and said, "Listen up, men. The order to ditch came from the President. All of you know what the drill is. Though we haven't been dropped into the drink before, we sure as hell know what it's like to be in and under it. I'll see you aboard one of the ships. Good luck."

"Good luck to you, Skipper," the men answered in unison.

Boxer returned to his seat.

Cowly followed him and said to Francine, "Miss Wheeler, please come with me."

Frightened, she managed to whisper, "I'm glad I met you, Jack, very glad." Then she left her seat and followed Cowly.

Standish came on the PA. "I have begun to dump fuel... The two ships are standing by... Everyone, put on your life jacket. Make sure it is securely tied. Do not inflate it until you have left the aircraft... Now remove your shoes... Place your seats in an upright position and lower your head, protecting it with your arms."

Boxer followed the instructions coming over the PA.

"We're going in!" Standish announced.

Boxer's heart raced. For a moment, his mind was a blank; then he thought about his son John. Though he had spoken to him on the phone, he hadn't seen him in almost a year. "If I survive this," he whispered, "I'll see him —"

The plane struck the water and bounced.

Boxer felt himself being pulled forward.

The plane slammed into the water again and jolted upward. The starboard wing ripped off.

Boxer was thrust back into the seat.

The plane crashed down into the water and quickly began to settle.

Boxer unbuckled his seat belt and rushed into the cockpit.

"We're okay," Standish said.

"Get the hell out!"

The three men hurried out of the cockpit and Boxer went after them.

"Skipper," Cowly shouted, "the men are out of the aircraft."

"Start moving the people," Boxer answered. "Move them out as fast as you can." He looked out of a window on either side of the aircraft. The exit was orderly.

"Skipper," one of the men on the outside shouted, "the boats are beginning to pick up survivors."

"She's settling fast," Boxer shouted to Cowly.

"Fifty or more people to go," Cowly said.

"Move them," Boxer answered. "Move them." He moved toward the emergency door on the portside.

"All passengers cleared," Cowly said.

"Get out," Boxer ordered. "Get out!" He turned and watched Cowly dive into the sea. Then he went out the door and onto the wing. There were people in life jackets all around.

The plane's tail began to slide under the waves.

Boxer dove into the sea and he surfaced just as the nose of the huge jet stood upright. An instant later the aircraft slid beneath the sunlit waves.

"This way," a man shouted.

Boxer turned and saw a lifeboat some distance from him. "Coming," he called. "I'm coming." And he began to swim toward the boat.

CHAPTER 5

Though the body of the man still lay twelve hundred feet under the surface of the North Atlantic, Boxer, his entire crew, and Sanchez listened to the high mass being said for De Vargas in the Church of the Sacred Heart. With the exception of himself and Cowly, no one else in the church knew that the body in the flag-draped sealed casket wasn't De Vargas. Kinkade had provided a body in a sealed casket.

The De Vargas family — Maria, the mother; Peter, the father; Diana, a twenty-two-year-old sister; twin teenaged brothers; and Nicole — were in the front center pew. Uncles, aunts, cousins, and friends filled the church.

Except for the evenings, Boxer had spent the last three days in the south Bronx with the family at their apartment or in the funeral home and had found them warm, loving, and truly grief-stricken. De Vargas was their miracle.

"And now," the priest said, "I call upon the one man, who knew our beloved son, Alvaro, perhaps better than anyone else, to say a few words about him to his family and friends — Captain Boxer."

Boxer stood up and walked slowly forward. Though he had known that he would be asked to speak, he hadn't prepared anything. He stopped in front of the casket and put his hand on it. That the real De Vargas was somewhere else didn't matter anymore. Boxer turned to the congregation and, looking toward the De Vargas family, said, "He was your son, your brother, and your sweetheart, Nicole, but he was our shipmate, our friend, and, to several of the men here, their commanding officer. He was a brave man, a very brave man.

He was a fair man. But most of all, he was a man in the truest sense of the word. In the past few days I learned that there were many, many different parts to him. I learned that though he was not a church-going man, he donated money to this church three times a year: Christmas, Easter, and Thanksgiving. The money bought food for the poor. The woman he intended to marry knows how brave he was. If it had not been for him, she would not be here today. He rescued her and her companions. Anything more I could say would be to no purpose. We loved and respected Alvaro." Having finished, Boxer faced the casket and saluted it. Then he walked slowly back to his place in his pew.

The cortege was very long. Boxer rode with Nicole in Sanchez's limo while the rest of the crew followed in rented cars. The Marine Corps provided an honor guard and, at the internment, fired the customary rounds and played taps.

Boxer took the folded flag from the Marine Sergeant and handed it to Mr. De Vargas who said, with tears streaming out of his eyes, "It will never be the same without him. Never!"

Boxer put his hands on the man's shoulders. "It won't be the same but he'd want you to make it better. Better for your other children and for Maria."

"First," Mr. De Vargas said, "I must find a way to live."

"You will. I'm sure you will," Boxer told him and with his arm around the man's shoulder, he led him to the waiting limo.

"Please, Captain, you and your men, come back to the apartment," Maria said, looking up at Boxer from the rear seat.

Though he wanted to return to Washington within the next few hours, he nodded and said, "Of course we'll come back."

"Thank you. Thank you," she answered.

Sipping a vodka on the rocks, Boxer stood near an open window. The apartment was crowded with people and was very hot. The furniture was scarred with age. On one wall was a large cross and on another a picture of the Virgin painted in bright colors on black velvet.

Ever since he and the other guests had arrived, platters of spicy-smelling food were being continually brought out from the kitchen and placed on the two bridge tables that had been set up in the living room. A makeshift bar, with an uncle doing the pouring and mixing, was set up in the entrance of the twins' bedroom.

Boxer looked down at the street. The sun had already passed it by, leaving it in shadow. From one end to the other, the tenement houses were all the same: five-floor walk-ups with fire escapes hanging on the front like the exoskeletons of some huge reptilian creatures that had climbed up the wall and had disappeared, leaving their bones behind. The street was littered with garbage. Groups of teenagers held court in front of the houses or leaned against the various parked cars.

"Not very pretty," a woman said.

Boxer turned and faced Diana. During the past few days, though courteous, she spoke to him only if he spoke to her. First he thought that she was shy, then that she was just an aloof person, and finally that she resented him because he was alive and her brother was dead. "Not pretty at all," he answered.

She held a drink in her hand and took a moment to sip it before she said, "Alvaro wanted us to move to a better neighborhood, but Mom and Dad — well, they had lived here since they came from Puerto Rico."

"It's hard for some people to make adjustments," Boxer said, aware that Diana was a beautiful woman, with dark eyes and long black hair.

"When you leave, may I come with you?" she asked.

Boxer raised his eyebrows.

"May I?" she asked, without giving any reason why she wanted to go with him.

"Yes. But I'm going back to the hotel."

"That's all right," Diana answered and walked away.

Boxer went to the bar for a refill; then eased his way back to the open window. Though he had wanted to return to Washington that day, or at least that evening, he now realized he was just too tired to travel and decided to stay another couple of days. Hopefully, it would give him the opportunity to see his son, John, and the Spadaro boy, Chuck.

Boxer was certain that Trish wouldn't like this new delay, but if he took the time now to see his son and Chuck, he would have more time with her later. He planned to take her to some resort and do nothing but rest and make love. He hoped she'd understand, but his conversations with her made him question whether the relationship was worth continuing. He always came to the conclusion that he was overreacting. He couldn't possibly expect her to know where he had been and how he felt, when he had told her nothing. He hadn't even told her that De Vargas had been killed. The problem was his, he decided. Not hers. Yet he could not help but think that, if she had joined him when he had asked her to, the experience of the last few days would have drawn them much closer together.

Boxer sighed softly and, finishing his drink, was about to look at the street again when Sanchez came up to him. "Would you like a ride downtown?"

"I'll stay a while longer," Boxer answered.

Sanchez looked toward the couch where Maria and Peter were sitting. "How's the family fixed?" he asked.

"There'll be money from the insurance," Boxer answered. "But that's not much. He just about supported them."

"I'll cover it," Sanchez told him. "But I don't want them to know where it's coming from."

"I was going to do the same," Boxer said, surprised at Sanchez's generosity. He and Sanchez had started out as adversaries, but now they had a friendship that ran deep.

"Between the insurance and what we give them, life should be somewhat easier."

Boxer agreed.

"If it hadn't been for me, the Lieutenant would be here now."

"Morell is the Company's responsibility," Boxer said tightly, "and the Company will take care of it."

"No," Sanchez said, "I will take care of it, or we will take care of it, but the Company won't."

"Find him and I'll take him out myself," Boxer said, his voice hardening.

"I'll call you," Sanchez said with a nod.

Boxer returned the gesture and faced the window. Across the street and below, the light from the apartments touched the fire escapes. Here and there a bare-chested man sat drinking a bottle of beer. And on the sidewalk, men were already playing cards on makeshift tables of empty wooden fruit boxes.

"I'm ready to go," Diana said.

Boxer turned. She was wearing a black cocktail dress with a princess collar instead of the one with a high collar she had worn for the funeral. "I want to say goodbye to your folks and Nicole."

"I'm going to get something cold to drink," she said. "I'll meet you at the door."

Boxer put his plastic glass down on the windowsill and went directly to where Maria and Peter were sitting.

Peter started to stand.

"No, please, don't get up," Boxer said. "Please."

"Captain," Maria said, "it was so good of you and your men to come."

"It couldn't have been any other way," Boxer replied, and he bent down and kissed the woman on the cheek."

"*Vaya con Dios,*" Maria said.

"Thank you. I'll come see you again," Boxer told her; then he shook Peter's hand. "If you need —"

"Nothing," Peter said, shaking his head. "You and the men have already given so much to my family. My son was buried with honor, and I couldn't ask for anything more."

"Your son lived with honor," Boxer responded.

"Yes, he lived with honor," Peter said with tears streaming down his face.

Boxer moved to Nicole. He reached down and gathered her into his arms. "Take care of yourself," he said.

"Thank you for everything you've done."

"No thanks needed. I'll see you in Washington," he said and kissed her on the lips before he let go of her.

"You're a good man, Captain, a very good man."

Boxer flushed. "Thank you," he said, turned, and walked to the door where Diana was already waiting.

During the cab ride down from the south Bronx, neither of them spoke; but she sat so close to Boxer that he could feel her thigh against his and the pressure of her breast against his arm.

And now they sat at a small, round table in the cocktail lounge of the hotel where Boxer was staying. The room was dimly lit and a candle in a green bowl cast a wavering light over the table, leaving their faces in shadow.

Boxer munched on a small pretzel, waiting for Diana to give some indication as to why she wanted to be with him. Her silence allowed him time to be occupied with his own thoughts, some of which concerned Morell. If Sanchez didn't find him, somehow he would himself and then he would kill him. No, he would damage him, just the way he did those bastards who mugged and then beat his mother to death. He took another pretzel and devoured it with a single ferocious bite.

"Angry?" Diana asked.

Boxer was caught off guard, but rather than lie, he nodded. "Very angry," he said.

"I have some questions, Captain, that might make you angrier," she said.

His stomach tightened. "If I can answer them, I will."

"My brother was no longer in the marines, yet the marines supplied an honor guard."

"They'll do that for all ex-marines," Boxer explained. "And your brother was proud of having been a marine."

Diana nodded and asked, "How did Alvaro die?"

Boxer took a deep breath and slowly exhaled. "One of those freak accidents that sometimes happen aboard ship or, for that matter, anywhere else."

"Captain —"

"Please, call me Jack," Boxer said.

Diana nodded. "All right, Jack, that doesn't answer the question."

This young woman was turning out to be tougher than Boxer had expected. She was a lot like Alvaro in that way. "He was underwater doing some repair work when an explosion occurred."

"Was that why the coffin was sealed?"

"He wasn't a pretty sight when he was brought to the surface."

Though her hand was trembling, she managed to pick up the glass and finish her drink.

"Another one?" Boxer asked.

"No, thank you. Two is my limit."

"Any more questions?"

"One," she pressed. "No, two."

"Ask," Boxer said.

"Why was your entire crew flown to New York?"

Boxer almost breathed a sigh of relief. He thought she might ask for the name of the ship and then he would have been forced to invent a story to explain why he and the crew were no longer on the *Tecumseh*. But he still wasn't off the hook: that might be her second question. "There was some hull damage and the ship had to go into dry dock for repairs that will take several weeks to complete. There really wasn't any reason to keep the crew aboard."

After a few moments, she said, "I guess I'll have to accept your story, won't I?"

"I guess you will," Boxer answered, still wondering what the second question would be.

Diana fished a cigarette case out of her bag, opened it, and held it out to Boxer.

"I smoke a pipe," he said, "and on certain occasions a cigar." He struck a match for her.

She took several deep drags and let the smoke rush out of her nostrils, before she quietly said, "Would you take me to your room?"

"What did you say?"

More smoke rushed from her nostrils. "Would you take me to your room?" she repeated.

"I'm flattered," Boxer said, "but it would serve no purpose."

"Do you understand what I want —"

Boxer held up his hand. "I understand, Diana. I really do understand."

"Don't you find me attractive?"

"You're more than attractive. You're beautiful. But the answer is still no."

"Because I am Alvaro's sister?"

"Yes. And because you're under an emotional strain and —"

She leaned across the table. "I'm not a virgin. I haven't been since I was fifteen."

"The answer is still no," Boxer said.

She leaned back into her seat. "I wanted to give you the only gift I can give."

Boxer reached across the table and took hold of her hand. "You don't have to give me anything."

Suddenly her young face wrinkled and she began to weep. "Alvaro was our prince. Our hero. Our provider. Now, we have no one to take care of us. I don't think there's even enough money to pay next month's rent."

Boxer squeezed her hand. "Trust me," he said. "Money won't be a problem."

"We never had —"

"Trust me," Boxer repeated, letting go of her hand to give her a handkerchief. "You and your family will not want for anything."

"But how —"

"No questions. Wipe the tears from your eyes and then go to the powder room. When you come back, I'll take you to dinner. Okay?"

"Okay," she echoed and, handing the handkerchief back to him, she stood up. "I'll be right back."

"Take your time," Boxer said.

She managed a smile and left the table.

Boxer watched the rolling movement of her buttocks as she walked and decided that he must be getting old, or, for reasons unknown to him, turning moral. But after a few moments' reflection he rejected both possibilities. Though he really didn't understand what it was, something else was stopping him from taking Diana to bed.

"Ready," Diana announced, returning to the table.

"Good. I'm starved," Boxer said. "How about Japanese food?"

"I never ate it."

"Then it's time you did," Boxer answered. He summoned the barmaid and paid the check. A short time later, with Diana on his arm, he left the cocktail lounge and walked out onto the street.

It was just past eight o'clock in the evening when Kinkade met Trish at the bar of the Sportsman Club, a restaurant in Falls Church, Virginia. Though happy to be out of the hot, humid night, he was anxious about meeting his granddaughter.

"I'm sorry I'm late," he said, accepting her kiss on the cheek. "There's always some last-minute crisis that has to be dealt with."

Trish nodded understandingly and, with a wry smile, she said, "We all know how you love saving the world."

"Let's sit down at a table where we'll be able to talk," Kinkade said.

"Sounds ominous," Trish responded.

"Serious would be a more accurate description," Kinkade said.

Trish nodded, slid off the stool, and, with her Rob Roy in hand, she walked alongside her grandfather.

"Have you heard from Boxer?" Kinkade asked.

"He calls every night," she answered. "I was expecting him back late this afternoon, but no doubt something else came up."

"Trish, you know my feelings toward Boxer, but in all fairness to him, you must understand that he hasn't exactly been on a pleasure trip," Kinkade said.

Trish didn't answer.

As Kinkade steered Trish toward a table near the window, the maître d' intercepted them and said, "I'm sorry, sir, that table is reserved."

Kinkade glared at the man. He was too angry to allow himself to be bullied by anyone. "That table does not have a reserved sign on it," he said stiffly. "That table is the one I want and if you give me one more word of nonsense about it being reserved, I will have you fired."

The man looked at Trish.

The best she could do was roll her eyes.

"Your table," the maître d' said, gesturing them toward it.

Kinkade helped Trish with the chair and then sat down himself.

A waiter came. "Dinner?" he asked.

"Have you had dinner?" he asked his granddaughter.

She shook her head.

"Dinner for two," Kinkade said.

"Would you care for something to drink?" the waiter asked.

"I'll have another Rob Roy," Trish said.

"A very dry martini with an olive," Kinkade told the waiter.

Trish waited until the waiter left the table; then she said, "You seem particularly irascible tonight."

"Comes with the turf, as they say," Kinkade replied.

Trish didn't answer.

Their drinks were set down in front of them and Kinkade picked his up first. "To good health and good luck," he toasted.

Trish touched her glass to his and drank.

"Aren't you going to make a toast?" Kinkade asked.

"The toast you made covers all the ground," she responded. "Anything more might anger the gods."

The waiter returned with the menus.

Kinkade put on his half-glasses in order to be able to read it. "What are you going to order?" he asked, peering at Trish around the side of the menu.

"A salad," she said.

"Bah, I want something more substantial than rabbit food," he told her.

"Then by all means, order it."

Kinkade looked at his watch. "Too late to eat meat and I'm not particularly keen on fish tonight. A salad might be the thing. Do they make good salads here?" Again he looked at her from the side of the menu.

"Very good," Trish answered, managing not to smile.

"I'll have whatever you're having," Kinkade said, closing the menu and putting it to one side of the table. "What are you having?"

"A Caesar salad."

"That's one of the few I like," Kinkade said, picking up his martini.

The waiter returned and Kinkade ordered, "A Caesar salad for two and don't stint on the anchovies."

"I'll see that you have a double portion," the waiter said.

"Cranky," Trish said, when the waiter was gone. "You're just cranky."

"That's part of my charm," Kinkade answered.

Trish uttered a snort of disdain.

"Are you going to marry Boxer?" Kinkade asked abruptly.

"I thought we agreed not to discuss that," Trish said.

"That was when you weren't sleeping with Captain Igor Borodine," Kinkade said.

Trish flushed. "I don't sleep with him," she said; then she added, "We're lovers."

"And what the hell is that supposed to mean?"

"Did you have me followed?"

"Answer my question: what does being lovers mean, other than that you go to bed with him?"

"He's a very remarkable man," Trish said.

"And you're a very remarkable woman to be able to give yourself to two men who are enemies."

"I won't even bother to comment on that."

"But it is true," Kinkade said.

"Did you have me followed?"

"I had him followed," Kinkade said. "My God, girl, have you any idea what you're doing?"

Trish remained silent.

"Do you know what will happen if his people find out?" Kinkade asked. "Well, I don't know either. But if the situation were reversed and I could get my claws into the son or daughter of the KGB, I'd have a field day."

"No one has their claws in me," Trish said defensively.

"Not yet."

"I love him," Trish said, "and I love Jack."

Kinkade finished his drink. "I could use another one of these," he said. "After listening to you, one isn't enough."

"I promise you, I'll sort it all out."

Kinkade shook his head. "Do you intend to marry Boxer?"

"I think both of us have doubts," she said.

"What if Boxer should find out about you and Borodine?" Kinkade asked.

"He won't, if you don't tell him, or if your agents don't tell him."

The waiter brought a huge wooden salad bowl to the table. "There is an extra portion of anchovies in the salad," he said, using a combination of spoon and fork to move some salad from the bowl to Trish's plate, then to Kinkade's.

"My life is my own," Trish said, as soon as the waiter had left and was out of earshot.

"Not as much your own as you want to believe," Kinkade answered, as he impaled some salad with his fork. "Your grandfather just happens to be the head of this country's intelligence operation. The KGB might try to do a great many things to compromise my position. They might even hold you hostage."

"That's absurd!"

"Extreme, yes, but certainly within the realm of possibility."

"I promise you we'll be very, very careful."

"What are you going to do when Boxer comes back?" Kinkade asked.

"Nothing."

"I don't understand what you mean by 'nothing'," Kinkade said.

"Many women have two lovers," Trish replied.

"I definitely need another drink!" Kinkade exclaimed and getting the waiter's attention he told him, "I want a double martini and make it very, very dry."

"Anything for the lady?" the waiter asked.

"Some morals," Kinkade growled.

"Grandpa!" Trish exclaimed.

"All right, I'm sorry. Bring her another one of whatever she was drinking," Kinkade said.

The motel was off I-95 in Maryland. The room was at the end of a line of rooms. Cowly unlocked the door, stepped inside, and switched on the light. The room was clean and cheerful looking with a floral wallpaper and rustic-type furniture. One green-and-white-curtained window looked out on the court and the other faced a small stand of woods.

"Looks fine to me," Cowly said.

"Me, too," Cynthia answered.

Cowly closed the door and put their bags on the luggage racks.

"I'd like to shower," Cynthia said. "Even in an air-conditioned car, I feel gritty after a long drive."

"I could use a shower myself," he answered.

"I won't be long," Cynthia said, as she took her toothbrush and toothpaste out of her nylon bag.

Cowly went to the window overlooking the woods and closed the blinds; then he did the same to the blinds on the front window. The sudden sound of the shower made him turn toward the closed bathroom door. That Cynthia was naked behind that door and that soon she would be coming back panicked him. His heart raced and he was sweating. What was he doing there? He hadn't been with a woman for five, maybe six years. And though he was very attracted to Cynthia, he still wasn't sure that he could satisfy her or that she would be able to satisfy him.

The shower stopped and Cynthia called out, "I'll be finished in a couple of minutes."

"No need to rush," Cowly answered, and telling himself that everything would be all right, he began to undress.

"Done," Cynthia said, opening the door and coming into the bedroom.

Cowly looked at her. A white terry towel was wrapped around her body and was secured by a knot over her breasts. By any standard, she was a stunningly beautiful woman.

"Anything wrong?" Cynthia asked.

Cowly shook his head. "You're beautiful," he said in a choked voice.

"I'm glad you think so," she replied with a smile. "I left you just enough hot water for a quick shower."

Cowly undressed down to his skivvies, took his shaving kit into the bathroom and after cleaning his teeth went into the shower. The hot water pouring over him felt good and eased some of the tension.

A few minutes later, Cowly shut the water off, stepped out of the shower, and began drying himself. When he had finished, he wrapped a towel around his waist. After a moment's hesitation, he opened the door.

Cynthia was in bed, resting on a pillow. The sheet was drawn over her breasts. Only the night-table lamp nearest her was on.

She patted the bed alongside of her. "Join me," she said.

Cowly crossed the room. He stood very still at the side of the bed. His heart was thumping.

She pulled back the sheet. "Come," she said in a low voice.

Cowly swallowed.

She was naked. "Come," she repeated.

Cowly pulled the towel off his waist, let it fall to the floor, and climbed into the bed.

She let the sheet drop on him.

The warmth of her body washed over him.

"We should talk," Cynthia said.

Cowly swallowed again and said, "Yes."

She turned to him. "First, hold me. Put your arms around me."

He faced her and drew her to him. Her body was delightfully soft and smelled good. Because he knew she wanted to be kissed, he kissed her. He had kissed her many times before, but never before had they been naked in bed.

Her body pressed gently against his. "You feel good," she said.

"You do too," Cowly answered.

"Are you sorry —"

"No. No. It's just that you're the first woman I've been with in years. I'm not sure of myself — Cynthia, I like you — No, it's more than like — Much more."

She ran her fingers through his hair. "If I didn't have more than just 'like' feelings for you, I wouldn't be here now."

"I know that. That's why I'm frightened out of my wits. I want to be the man you want."

"You are."

"You don't know that and I don't know that, at least not yet."

"Listen to me. I told you I was married and divorced."

"And that you have a daughter who lives with your mother."

"I've been around," she said. "Jack and I —"

"I know you were lovers," Cowly said.

"Off and on," she admitted.

"Do you still love him?" Cowly asked.

"Yes. I guess I always will. But not to sleep with him again."

"Even if he asked you to?"

Cynthia shook her head. "No, that's over. It's been over for some time now."

Cowly kissed her again. Then he said, "I'm glad I'm here with you."

Cynthia put her arms around him. "If I didn't think I could make you happy, I wouldn't have let things between us go this far."

"I know."

"Love me," she whispered.

CHAPTER 6

"Thanks for coming here," Kinkade said, looking across the desk at Admiral Stark.

Stark nodded. He preferred not to meet with Kinkade at Langley, but this was one of the times where his preference went by the boards.

Kinkade had called earlier in the day and had asked him to come to his office.

"I'd make the trip to yours," Kinkade had said, "but I'm feeling a bit under the weather."

That had been enough for Stark: he had agreed to go to Langley without requiring any additional explanation from Kinkade.

"We have two things to consider," Kinkade said. "One has to do with the *Tecumseh* and the other with Boxer."

"Let's deal with Boxer first," Stark responded in his gravelly voice. From past experience he knew that anytime Kinkade wanted to talk about Boxer, it meant that Boxer had done something that Kinkade disapproved of.

Kinkade opened a humidor and offered Stark a cigar. "Go ahead, take one," he urged. "They're Cuban. I can't smoke them since my heart attack."

Stark ran the cigar under his nose. "Good," he said. "Very good."

"If you like it, I'll send half-a-dozen boxes over to your office."

"How did you manage to get Cuban cigars?" Stark asked, lighting up.

Kinkade grinned. "I have friends in Cuba," he said.

"Translated," Stark said, "that means you have agents there."

Kinkade shrugged.

"Let's get on with Boxer," Stark said, blowing smoke off to the right.

Kinkade leaned back into the high-back leather chair. "This last mission didn't exactly turn out the way we had hoped."

"We?" Stark questioned.

"Only in the editorial sense. It turned out to be exceedingly costly in men and equipment."

"Tell me about it," Stark said, puffing on the cigar. "We lost almost an entire strike force. De Vargas died as a result of injuries he had sustained during the attack and the *Turtle* had to be destroyed. We couldn't salvage her."

Kinkade opened the top drawer on the left side of the desk and took out a hard candy wrapped in cellophane. "Sugarless," he explained. "Believe me, it doesn't take the place of a good cigar."

"Very few things do," Stark replied.

"There were two parts to that mission," Kinkade said, popping the candy into his mouth.

Stark leaned slightly forward. "What was the second part?"

"That was strictly an agency operation," Kinkade said, "and I might add a very successful one."

Stark was beginning to feel very uneasy. He forced himself to remain seated.

"Boxer tried to kill Bruno Morell," Kinkade said. "He has sent a message to me demanding that I have Morell killed."

"In his place," Stark said, "I don't doubt that I'd have done the same thing. The man —"

"Was following orders," Kinkade said, bouncing forward and putting his elbows on the desk.

Stark took the cigar out of his mouth. "I'm not sure I understand you."

"The attack on the fortress was completely diversionary. It permitted agents already in place to get the people out."

"Morell knew this?" Stark asked.

Kinkade nodded.

"Did he or did he not set up Boxer's men?"

"I don't like to use the expression 'set up.' The man —"

Stark was on his feet. "A hundred men were killed to get how many out?"

"Two."

"Two!" Stark repeated. "Two!"

"I assure you," Kinkade said, unwrapping another candy, "they are worth —"

"You tell the mothers, wives, sweethearts, fathers, and children of the men who were killed that two men were worth their loss."

"These men are specialists. They were needed by our scientists."

"How the hell did the Libyans get hold of them?"

"They kidnapped them from an international conference in Rome."

"I wouldn't ever tell this to Boxer," Stark said. "He just might kill you."

"That's what you'd like to do, isn't it?"

"Kinkade, let me tell you a story. This goes back many, many years when I was still in high school. My uncle taught history at the school. He was a good teacher. In one of his classes, an honor class, there was a young man who really wasn't doing the work. He'd come to class and put his head down on the desk. My uncle called the boy's parents and he was told by the boy's mother that the boy had a very heavy sports schedule.

When the end of the term came, my uncle gave the boy a seventy-five, which was a very low grade for a student in an honor class. The boy's mother called and demanded the mark be changed. My uncle refused."

"What's the point of the story?" Kinkade asked.

"Let me finish," Stark said, still standing. "It has a point. A year later the boy's mother became the president of the Parent-Teacher Association and the first thing she did was go to the school's principal and demand that the grade be changed. The principal called my uncle down to the office and, after giving him the standard bullshit about how much he admired him, he asked him to change the boy's grade. My uncle maintained that the boy's work and attitude was far below the rest of the class. But the principal said it was important to understand that the boy was in an honor track and the mark my uncle gave him would certainly affect his average when it came time for the boy to apply to college. Then my uncle made the mistake of thinking that the principal would understand that it would be immoral to raise the boy's mark without raising the marks of all the students and said as much. The principal didn't have any concept of what was moral or immoral. He wanted to satisfy the boy's mother and without a moment's hesitation, he said, 'Raise all of the marks.'"

"What did your uncle do?"

"Having suggested that all the marks be raised, he couldn't very well back down when the principal agreed to it."

"I'm not sure I understand the relationship between your story and —"

"One hundred men died to save two men; the marks of thirty-five students were raised because the mother of one boy wanted her son's mark raised. Both situations are glaring examples of the abuse of power."

"Are you saying that I abused —"

"Kinkade, someone did," Stark said. "Someone certainly made the decision to use Morell."

"I did," Kinkade responded.

Stark sat down. "Unless you tell Boxer the truth about the mission, he won't be satisfied until Morell is taken out. But if you tell him, he'll probably try to kill you."

"I can't tell him."

"Whether you do or not is up to you," Stark said, relighting the dead cigar.

"There's something else."

Stark raised his eyebrows questioningly.

"Morell is well connected in certain circles."

"Meaning?" Stark asked.

"The Mafia."

Stark blew a cloud of smoke toward the ceiling. "Then pass the word to them — and I know you can — to watch their asses. Boxer can be one mean bastard."

"Try to talk him out of going after Morell," Kinkade said.

"I'd be wasting my time," Stark said. "If he chooses not to do anything, the choice will be his. Nothing I or anyone else can say will make the slightest bit of difference. You should know by this time, Boxer is completely his own man."

Kinkade sighed and shook his head. "His own man and my problem," he said.

"What about the *Tecumseh*?" Stark asked, wanting to change the subject.

"That's exactly what I wanted to ask you," Kinkade said. "She seems to have completely vanished. I was sure one of your submarines would at least ID the sound of propellers."

"Nothing," Stark answered, shaking his head.

"I'd still bet that the Russians have her," Kinkade said.

"If they do, they've stashed her away where we can't find her."

"That's for sure!" Kinkade agreed.

"Well, I guess that wraps it up," Stark said, starting to stand.

"There's one more thing," Kinkade told him.

Stark settled in the chair again.

"I'm going to retire. My heart is giving me more trouble and my doctor said I can't really take the stress of the job."

"I'm sorry you're being forced to go," Stark said.

"So am I. So am I."

"When will you be leaving?"

"The end of the month," Kinkade said. "The President has already accepted my resignation, but nothing has been said to the press about it yet."

"Any idea who'll be your successor?"

"None."

Stark puffed on the cigar. "Any plans?"

"Nothing beyond taking life easy," Kinkade said. "Maybe I'll do a bit of traveling."

Stark stood up and offered his hand. "Good luck," he said.

"Trish said something about having dinner, but she wants to wait until Boxer returns."

"He's coming back in a day or two," Stark said.

"I'll leave it to Trish to set it up," Kinkade answered.

"By the way," Stark asked, "are those two going to marry?"

"I never know what Trish is going to do," Kinkade said. "She's becoming more and more unpredictable. The answer is: I don't know."

Stark accepted the statement without any change of expression, but he could tell from the sound of Kinkade's voice that he was pissed, really pissed at his granddaughter.

Boxer leaned forward. "The house on the right," he told the driver.

"Yes, sir," the driver answered, slowing the government limo and finally stopping it. A few moments later he opened the rear door for Boxer.

"Wait outside the car," Boxer said, looking across the street where a group of four boys were standing. "Those little bastards could probably strip this in a matter of minutes."

The driver grinned. "In about five they'd be off with the stereo, the tape deck, and the hub caps."

Boxer agreed and said, "Look mean."

"I'll do my best," the man said, highballing Boxer.

Boxer returned the salute and walked toward the house. He went up the two steps and was about to knock at the door when Rose opened it.

"Captain Boxer," she exclaimed, fluttering her eyelashes at him. "I didn't expect you so quickly. Come in."

"Not much traffic," Boxer lied as he entered the foyer. He had called earlier in the morning and had told Chuck to be ready about two. "Where is he?"

"I told him what you said," she answered.

"Where is he?" Boxer asked, sensing trouble.

"Here I am," Chuck said, coming down the steps.

Boxer looked at him. He was wearing jeans, a T-shirt, and a red band around his head. The jeans and the T-shirt were dirty. "I told you to be dressed by the time I came."

"I'm dressed."

Boxer looked at Rose. "Has he got a pair of regular pants, a white shirt, and a sports jacket. And a pair of shoes?"

Before she could answer, Chuck said, "Yeah, I have them."

"Good. Then get your ass into them now!" Boxer ordered. "Do it, or I'll dress you myself. And shower and shave before you dress. Move it. You have ten minutes. At the end of that time, if you're not down here fully dressed, I'll come upstairs and help you."

Chuck was about to complain.

Boxer moved toward him. "Don't push it," he said in a low angry voice.

Chuck turned and ran upstairs.

"Captain, would you like a beer?" Rose asked.

Boxer turned to her. "Yes, a beer would be fine."

"I'll get it from the fridge," she said. "You sit down in the living room and make yourself at home."

Boxer followed her into the kitchen. "Where's Vinny?" he asked, referring to the man with whom she was living the last time he met her.

"Bad, that one," she said, taking two bottles of beer out of the fridge, opening both, and handing Boxer one of them. "As soon as you left the last time, he wanted to start trouble."

Boxer drank the beer out of the bottle.

"He got real itchy about the money," Rose said.

"Happens," Boxer answered.

"I mean, after all Chuck is my sister's boy. He's my blood. Know what I mean?"

"I know what you mean."

She smiled at him.

"How is he doing in school?" Boxer asked.

"Don't ask."

"I just did," Boxer said. "I want to know."

"He cuts. How can he do anything when he's not there?"

"Still playing games, eh!" Boxer commented.

"He's wild and —"

"I'm dressed," Chuck said, coming into the kitchen.

Boxer checked his watch. "Nine minutes," he said, looking at the boy. "Not bad. You might even pass yourself off as a member of the human race."

"Do I have to wear the jacket. It's hot and —"

"When I take mine off," Boxer told him, "you can take yours off." Then he thanked Rose for the beer and said, "I'll bring him back sometime tonight."

"Be good," she called after Chuck.

Boxer opened the door and stepped through the doorway. The group of boys, who had been across the street, had moved into the gutter and were now standing directly in front of the limo.

"Hey, guys, look at Chucky," one of them called.

"He's all duded up for the admiral," another said.

The group suddenly moved between Boxer and the limo.

"You a real sailor," a boy asked, "or just a fake."

Boxer stopped. "Listen, punks, either you move aside, or I'll send each of you to the hospital."

"Maybe you'll be goin' to the hospital," one of them said, suddenly brandishing a switchblade.

"Mistake," Boxer said, "big mistake." And he leaped forward, kicking the boy with the knife in the face.

"Christ!" one of the other boys shouted as the driver struck him from behind.

The other two boys backed away.

"Want more?" Boxer asked.

The boys didn't answer.

"Captain, we've got company," the driver said and gestured up the street. Two men holding baseball bats were running toward them.

"Shit!" Boxer exclaimed.

"We can try to get the hell out of here," the driver said.

"No. I'll be coming back from time to time and I don't want to have to deal with this kind of crap."

"Hey creep," one of the men shouted, "I'm goin' to beat your brains out." Then to the other man, he said, "Sal, get the windshield."

Boxer bent down and pulled a snub-nosed .38 from a leg holster. "Freeze!" he said.

The two men stopped.

"Now listen and listen good. If you know any of these punks—"

"The boy you hit is my son," one of the men said.

"The boy I hit pulled a knife," Boxer said. "Now all of you listen up."

"Who do you think you're talkin' to?" the other man asked.

"I said 'listen'," Boxer answered in a flat, angry voice. "Listen, because if you don't, you're going to be in trouble. First, Chuck is my responsibility. Anything happens to him and I'll be after you. Get that through your thick skulls. Next, my name is Captain Jack Boxer. I won't tell you what my job is, but I will tell you that I can, with one call on the radio, have this entire street sealed off so that not even the cops can get in or out until I say so."

"You're full of shit!" the father said. "Nobody can do that."

Boxer looked at the driver. "Send a code ten to the base."

"Aye, aye, sir," the driver answered. He dropped into the front seat and picked up the mike.

"He's bluffing," the same man said.

Boxer looked at his watch. "Three to five minutes before the helicopters show," he said, realizing that almost everyone who lived on the street was outside.

"On their way," the driver said, getting out of the car.

Suddenly two marine helicopters came in off the bay. One took a position at one end of the street; another at the other end. Then above the sound of their engines a voice came over a PA system. "This street is sealed off. No one will be permitted to leave or enter until further notice." The message was repeated three times.

Two troop-carrying helicopters arrived. Marines leaped from the ships and immediately deployed along the street.

"For Christsakes he's brought the fuckin' marines out!" one of the men said.

A lieutenant came up to Boxer, saluted, and said, "The men are in position, sir."

Boxer nodded. "Thank you, Lieutenant," he said. "The threat no longer exists. You can recall your men."

The lieutenant saluted.

Boxer returned the salute.

"Saddle up," the lieutenant shouted to his men. "Saddle up!"

"Radio the helicopters to withdraw," Boxer said.

"Yes, sir," the driver answered.

"This street is now open," the pilot of one of the helicopters said over the PA. "This street is now open."

Boxer slipped the .38 back into its holster, and straightening up, looked at the two men. "Do you understand?"

Both nodded.

"Good," Boxer said. "Very good. I'm glad because I don't want trouble every time I come here."

"Who the hell are you?" one of the men asked.

"I already told you. Captain Jack Boxer," he said, Then turning to Chuck, he told him to get into the car. A moment later, he sat down next to the boy.

"I don't believe what happened," Chuck said. "I don't fuckin' believe it."

"Nothing happened," Boxer said with a straight face. "Nothing really happened.'"

"You've got to be kidding!" Chuck responded.

Boxer turned to the driver. "Did anything happen?" he asked.

"No, sir," the driver answered. "Nothing happened."

Chuck shook his head. "I don't fuckin' believe it."

"Believe it," Boxer said. "Believe it!"

The limo pulled up in front of the new apartment building on the east side.

"I'll be here for a while," Boxer told the driver.

"I don't have anywhere special I want to go," the man said, "but I might want to take a walk in the park."

Boxer nodded. "No problem. Check with me when you come back. I'll be in apartment two two C."

"Yes, sir," the driver answered, getting out to open the door for Boxer and Chuck.

"Who lives here?" Chuck asked, as they headed into the lobby.

"My ex-wife and my son," Boxer said.

A uniformed doorman stopped them. "Who —"

"Mrs. Gwen —" He had forgotten the name of the doctor she had married and then divorced. Instead of the name, he offered, "Apartment twenty two C."

He picked up the phone and checked. "You're expected. Go right in," the doorman said.

"Class," Chuck commented, as they went toward the elevator. Then he asked. "How old is your boy?"

"Ten or eleven."

"Don't you know which?"

"No," Boxer said quietly. "I don't."

"Some father you are," Chuck said accusingly.

Boxer didn't answer. He hadn't seen John or Gwen for the better part of a year. She didn't come to his father's or mother's funeral and she wouldn't let John come either. The doctor she married had something to do with it, but Boxer couldn't remember what. Suddenly, he was nervous.

The elevator came and its door opened.

"My son's name is John," Boxer said, as they started up.

"Yeah, at least you remembered that," Chuck said sullenly. "All you sea guys are alike. You drop your load in some dame. A kid is born. Your kid, and you can't even remember how old the kid is."

Boxer put his hand on Chuck's shoulder. "It's not —"

"Sure it is," Chuck said, pulling away. "Sure it is. Did you bring the kid anything?"

Stunned by Chuck's reaction, Boxer shook his head.

"You can call out the fuckin' marines, but you can't even buy your kid a toy."

The elevator stopped and the two of them walked out into the hallway.

"It's to the right. The last apartment," Boxer said. Chuck followed him.

"Are you going to be all right?" Boxer asked, just before he rang the bell.

"Yeah. Yeah. I won't spoil nothin'."

Boxer stabbed the bell with his forefinger. His stomach balled up into a knot. The door opened and he found himself looking at Gwen. She wore a pair of light-blue slacks, a white polo shirt, and no bra. Her black hair was tied back with a white ribbon, she hadn't changed much. She was still a beautiful woman.

"Come in," she said, swinging the door wide.

"Gwen, Chuck. Chuck, Gwen," Boxer said, as soon as they were in the apartment.

"Hello, Chuck," Gwen said offering her hand.

Chuck shook it.

"Where's John?" Boxer asked.

"Watching cartoons on TV in his room," Gwen answered.

"Did you tell him I was coming?"

"No. I wanted it to be a surprise," she said.

The three of them advanced toward the boy's bedroom. Boxer glanced around. Many of the paintings on the wall were familiar and some of the furniture was too, but much of it was new. Gwen seemed to change apartments and their decor whenever she changed husbands or lovers.

Suddenly Chuck said, "Aren't you on TV — on that soap — "

"Yes," Gwen laughed. "That's me."

"You never told me she was an actress," Chuck said, looking at Boxer.

"He just doesn't like to remember it," Gwen commented.

Boxer let the gibe pass. He wasn't going to argue about something they had argued about too many times before.

"Why don't you go in first," Gwen suggested, taking hold of Chuck's arm.

Boxer flashed her a grin. "Okay with you, Chuck?" he asked.

"Okay."

Boxer entered the room alone.

John was stretched out on the floor. He was too intent on watching TV to glance over his shoulder to see who had entered the room. "That you, Mom?" he asked.

Boxer was surprised by how much his son had changed since he had seen him last. The boy was still tow-headed, but he was taller and broader.

Suddenly the screen went blank and the words *NEWS FLASH* filled the screen. The camera zoomed in on a young black woman. "This is a news flash from the Channel Two newsroom. About two hours ago Captain Steven Bush killed one man and injured two others in a daring escape from the Psychiatric Section of the Bethesda Naval Hospital in Bethesda, Maryland. Naval and civilian personnel are combing the area adjacent to the hospital in an effort to find Captain Bush. Authorities at the hospital warn that Captain Bush is very dangerous. More details during News at Five."

Stunned, Boxer was unaware that his son was looking at him. The cartoon resumed.

"Dad!" John exclaimed, scrambling to his feet.

Boxer recovered just in time to catch the boy in his arms. "Hey, boy, you're an armful," he said, hugging him tightly.

"Dad, Mom didn't tell me you were coming," John said.

"I told her not to. I wanted to surprise you."

"I missed you, Dad. I really missed you."

"And I missed you," Boxer said, feeling his throat tighten. He had been remiss. He should have come to see him sooner.

"Who's that?" John asked.

Boxer realized that Gwen and Chuck had come into the room. He put John down and, turning toward them, he said, "That's Chuck, a friend of mine. Chuck, this is my son, John."

"Hi," Chuck said.

"Hello," John answered.

"Well, boys, how do we spend the afternoon?" Boxer asked. "The two of you decide. The two of you talk it over. What about it?"

"That's okay with me," Chuck said.

"John?"

"All right."

"Come," Boxer said to Gwen, "we'll leave them."

As soon as they were out of the room, Gwen asked, "Would you like a drink?"

Boxer nodded. "I could use one."

Gwen went to the brass bar cart. "Vodka on the rocks?"

"Yes," Boxer nodded. He moved to the window and looked out over the park. He was concerned about Bush.

Gwen came up behind him.

He could smell her tea-rose perfume.

"Your drink," she said.

Boxer turned. She held a glass in each hand.

"Which is mine?" he asked.

She shook her head. "It makes no difference; they're both the same."

Boxer took the glass from her right hand.

"What shall we drink to?" Gwen asked.

"Good health and good luck."

"Why not," she answered. "To good health and good luck." And she entwined her arm with his.

"You're looking good," Boxer said, after he drank.

"I didn't think you had noticed," she responded.

Boxer let the remark pass. "John looks good too," he said, suddenly feeling constrained.

"What's wrong?" Gwen asked.

"Wrong?"

"Jack, I know all the signs," she said. "Remember, we were married for a few years."

"Nothing is —"

"You don't lie very well," she said, moving away from him.

Suddenly the intercom buzzed.

"Excuse me," Gwen said, going toward the phone.

"It's for me," Boxer told her.

She stopped, gave him a quizzical look, and said, "Then perhaps you should answer it."

Boxer went to the phone. "This is Captain Boxer," he told the doorman.

"Your driver wants to see you," the doorman said.

"Send him up and will you please keep an eye on the limo?"

"Yes."

Boxer put the phone down and returned to where he had left Gwen.

"Did you tell him to call?" she asked.

"No," Boxer said. "He called because he received a radio message."

"What's wrong?" Gwen asked.

"Nothing is —"

"I know all the signs," she said ruefully.

He managed a smile. "Be thankful then that you don't have to put up with them." He walked to the bar cart and poured himself another drink.

Gwen followed. "You didn't tell me about Chuck. Is he the son of —"

"He's Rugger's son," Boxer said, looking out of the window; then in a softer and sadder tone, he added, "Rugger is dead."

"How?"

Boxer shrugged but remained silent.

The doorbell chimed.

"I'll go," Boxer said.

"Suit yourself," Gwen answered.

Boxer went to the door and opened it.

"Sorry to bother you, sir," the driver said. "But a code nine response call came over the radio for you from Admiral Stark and a Mr. Kinkade."

Boxer nodded and, opening the door wider, asked the driver to come in. "Would you like a beer or something harder?"

"Thanks, but I'm not a drinking man."

"A soda then?"

"That would do fine."

"Come with me," Boxer said and he led the man into the living room. "My ex —"

"Mrs. Boxer," Gwen said.

The man nodded.

"He would like a glass of soda," Boxer said, surprised that Gwen had returned to using his name.

"Any special kind?" Gwen asked.

"Whatever you have, as long as it's cold."

"While you're getting the soda," Boxer said, "I'll use the phone in the bedroom."

Gwen headed for the kitchen.

A few moments later, Boxer sat down on Gwen's double bed and picking up the handheld set, he punched out the number of Stark's red phone.

"Stark here," the admiral answered in his gravelly voice.

Boxer identified himself.

"Captain Bush escaped," Stark said.

"I know. It came over the TV as a news flash."

"You know he killed —"

"Yes, I know."

"His doctors say he might go after you," Stark said.

"I thought about that."

"Do you think he will?"

"From his point of view, he certainly has cause."

"Anyone else Bush might go after?"

"Commanders Cowly and Lowe."

"Why those two?"

"Bush was or thought he was in love with Lowe. But Cowly — Admiral, it doesn't make sense to tell it this way."

"Where are they now?"

"On their way back to Washington," Boxer said.

"I'll make sure they're protected and, when you come in, I'll do the same."

Boxer was about to tell Stark that he didn't want a bodyguard, but he knew it would be useless.

"Where are you going to stay when you return?" Stark asked.

"With Trish," Boxer answered.

"I want you to stay somewhere else and that's an order. Take her with you. But I don't want you in her apartment, at least not for a while."

"Anything else?"

"Yes. Captain Borodine has been assigned to his country's embassy."

"That's great," Boxer exclaimed. "Really great!"

"What was that code ten call all about?" Stark asked.

"Some trouble in Staten Island."

"With Rugger's son?"

"The neighbors began to push. The easiest way to deal with it was to show them I could push a lot harder."

Stark laughed. "They must have shit a brick when they saw the marines come."

"They sure as hell did. They won't try to push again."

"When do you expect to return to Washington?"

"The first flight out tomorrow morning," Boxer said.

"Be at my office by eleven hundred," Stark told him. "I want to start your debriefing."

"I'll be there," Boxer said, then added, "Kinkade wants me to call him."

"And you prefer not to talk to him," Stark commented.

"Not unless it's important."

"Okay," Stark said, "I'll handle him."

"I appreciate that," Boxer responded.

"By the way," Stark said, "the President approved your promotion. As of yesterday, you're a real admiral."

"What about Cowly?"

"He's a captain now."

"Thanks. He really deserves it," Boxer said.

"My office. Eleven hundred," Stark told him.

"Aye, aye, sir," Boxer said and, putting the phone back in its housing, he stood up. That he had been given a star didn't seem to have much meaning — at least not yet. Maybe it would when he and Trish were together. But now —

Gwen walked into the bedroom. "You have that look again," she said.

He forced himself to smile. "Just a routine matter," he said.

"The boys want to go for a drive around the park," she told him. "Then to, of all places, Coney Island."

Boxer grinned. "I bet that was John's idea."

"How did you know that?"

"I told him about Coney Island," Boxer said proudly. "I told him that my father used to take me there when I was a boy."

"Well, he wants to go there now."

Boxer started for the door.

"Jack, are you coming back here tonight?" she asked.

"We'll probably —" Boxer faced her. He realized that she wanted him to spend the night with her.

Gwen flushed.

"There was a time," he said softly, "when I would have stood on my head to spend a night with you. But now I would be happy if we could just be friends."

"I understand," she answered. "I really do."

Boxer reached out and took hold of her hand. "Come," he said, "let's all go for a drive around the park and to Coney Island."

CHAPTER 7

Boxer was on the 7 A.M. flight to Washington. The day was clear and not as warm as the previous few days had been. He was looking forward to being with Trish and was feeling good about himself. He had done what he previously had thought he never would be able to do: he had turned down the opportunity to have sex with two different women for two different reasons. He had passed up the opportunity to go to bed with De Vargas's sister because he intuitively knew that she would have been sorry afterwards. With Gwen it had been totally different. He no longer had any feelings for her that way. He no longer loved her or wanted her to love him. He was just content to be her friend.

If Boxer was the least bit concerned about anything, it was about Bush. Not that he was afraid of him, but rather that the man had become a threat to other people. Boxer wasn't about to dwell on Bush. He was someone else's problem now — not his. He had had more than enough of him aboard the *Shark* and the *Turtle*.

Almost before Boxer realized it, the stewardess announced over the PA, "Ladies and gentlemen, we will be landing at Washington's International Airport in ten minutes. Please fasten your seat belts and observe the 'No Smoking' sign when it comes on. Thank you for flying Eastern Airlines this morning."

A short while later, Boxer was in a cab on his way to Trish's apartment. Because he wanted to surprise her, he didn't stop to phone her from the airport. And, more importantly, he was hoping to spend a few hours in bed with her before going to his meeting with Stark.

The doorman nodded to him and said, "Good morning."

Boxer returned the greeting and rode the elevator up to the twenty-fifth floor. Trish had bought the apartment after she'd divorced McElroy, and Boxer had moved in with her a month after that.

He stopped in front of the door, fished out the key, and unlocked the door. A few moments later he was inside. The sun was already streaming through the sliding glass door that opened onto the balcony. It felt good to be back, very good. He crossed the dining room and walked into the bedroom. Trish wasn't there! The bed was still made. He glanced at the digital clock on the night table. It was 0912:05.

Boxer looked around. It was obvious that the bedroom hadn't been used the previous night — perhaps for several nights? He walked back into the dining room and wondered where Trish might be. It was possible that she was visiting friends for a few days. She had many friends and almost all of them had summer homes either on the shore or in the western mountains of Virginia and Maryland. Kinkade had a place on the eastern shore of Virginia. She might have gone there. Washington wasn't the best place to stay during the summer. Suddenly he heard the doorknob turn.

Boxer looked toward the door.

A moment later, it opened and Trish walked in. "The doorman told me you were here," she said.

"I thought I'd surprise you," Boxer said, moving close to her, "but I was the one who was surprised."

"That's life, isn't it?" she said with a smile and, giving him a perfunctory kiss, she headed for the bedroom.

Boxer followed her. "I don't remember you telling me that you were going to spend a few days away," he said.

"I must have forgotten to mention it," she answered. "Well, anyway you were certainly too occupied to be interested in the unimportant details of my life."

"Trish, that's not fair. I haven't exactly been on a vacation," Boxer said.

Trish didn't answer.

"I have a meeting with Stark at eleven hundred," Boxer said. "I'll probably have to spend a few days in the city; then we should be free to go anywhere you want."

"Now I want a nice hot bath and a few hours' sleep," she told him.

"You look as if you haven't had much sleep," he commented.

"I didn't."

"Who were you visiting?" Boxer asked.

"You know I don't like questions," she said and began to undress.

Boxer watched her, aware that she was wearing a blue dress with nothing more than a very thin white bra and skimpy panties under it. He wasn't sure what he should do or say. She was certainly hostile. Perhaps hostile was too strong a word, but she definitely wasn't friendly.

Completely naked, Trish faced him. "Have you any idea when your meeting will be over?" she asked.

"None," Boxer said, forcing down the desire to sweep her into his arms.

"Come talk to me while I bathe," she said, going into the bathroom.

Boxer stood in the doorway while she turned the water on. The bathtub was large and recessed into the floor. To get into it, she had to step down.

"Grandpa didn't tell me, but from the few hints he did give, I gathered this last mission was hard," she said, settling into a mass of bubbles.

Boxer nodded.

"Was it hard?" she asked, using a washcloth on her body.

"Harder than I thought it would be," he said.

For several moments neither of them spoke.

Boxer was beginning to feel more and more ill at ease.

Trish was the first to speak. "I'm sorry about De Vargas," she said. "I know how much you thought of him and he of you."

"He was a good man and a good officer."

"Your Captain Borodine came to see you," Trish said, looking up at Boxer.

"Stark told me he was here. Did you get the chance to speak to him?"

"He didn't seem to want to talk to me," she lied. "I have a number where you can contact him. He said he'd be in Washington for a while."

"He's here as an adviser to the Russian delegation —"

"Spare me the details," Trish said. "All those international conferences bore me. Oh, there is one thing you might want to know about him."

"And what's that?"

"He's an admiral," she said.

"Ah, that's good. He deserves it. He's the best the Russians have got."

"Is that all you can say?" Trish asked.

"Stark told me I got my star too," he answered, suddenly feeling very foolish having told her about it now.

"You mean you're an admiral?"

"Yes," he said.

Trish made a humming sound. "You don't look very pleased about it," she said.

"I am. But —"

"Will you reach over and do my back?" she asked.

Boxer took off his jacket and placed it on the back of a chair. Then he rolled up his sleeves.

"Careful not to slip," Trish said, handing him the washcloth.

Boxer moved the soapy cloth over her back.

"Ah, that feels good!"

Extending his reach, Boxer slid the cloth over her breasts. "Does that feel good too?" he asked, kissing the wet back of her neck.

"You started to say 'but' something or other," Trish said.

"I don't remember," Boxer answered. "I guess it wasn't very important."

Trish stood up and, reaching for the water spray, she warned Boxer to step back. "I feel so much better after a bath," she said, stepping out of the tub and draping a large white towel over her shoulders.

Boxer came up behind her and ran his hands over her back and down her sides. She smelled of flowers. "I want you," he said huskily.

She leaned back against him. "I was beginning to get that idea," she answered in a low voice.

Boxer put his hands on her breasts and gently rubbed them with the towel. Then he rubbed her stomach.

"Why didn't you come back —" Trish began.

"Let's not discuss that now," Boxer said, using the towel to turn her toward him.

Trish closed her eyes and, tilting her head back, she offered him her lips.

Boxer kissed her softly, then more urgently.

"Finish drying me," she said, easing her face away from his.

Boxer knelt and moved the towel gently down her flanks and back up. "Dry," he said, burying his face in the hollow of her stomach.

She kissed the top of his head.

Boxer got to his feet, draped the towel around her shoulders, and picked her up in his arms. "I missed you," he said, carrying her into the bedroom.

Moments later he set her down at the side of the bed and, while she removed the spread, he undressed.

"We don't have all that much time," Trish said, climbing into the bed.

"Time enough," Boxer said, settling next to her and taking her into his arms. "I love you," he said, kissing her lips.

"I love you too," Trish closed her eyes. "I really do love you."

At the door of his office, Stark greeted Boxer with a vigorous handshake. "For someone who has done what you have done and been where you have been, you look remarkably well," Stark commented in his gravelly voice.

"Don't let looks deceive you," Boxer answered. "What you see on the outside is not on the inside."

"Suppose we get out of the office and go somewhere where we can have a leisurely lunch and talk," Stark suggested. "You haven't had lunch, have you?"

"And not much of a breakfast either," Boxer commented.

"Just give me a couple of minutes to clear my desk and we'll be on our way," Stark said, heading for his desk.

Boxer took a few minutes to look around the room. It was as spartan as the first time he had seen it. The photograph of the President hung on the wall behind Stark's desk. The American flag was to his right and his five-star flag stood on his left. Except for a few other photos of ships he had served on and the planes he had flown the other walls were bare. Everything else in the room was government issue, including the four leather chairs and round, oak coffee table which were off to one side of the room.

"Ready," Stark said, putting down the phone. "Even when I'm not here, I'm here. I have to let the DO know where I'm going." He flipped open a humidor and picked up four cigars. "Kinkade gave me these. He got them from his friends in Cuba."

"I'm glad he had friends somewhere," Boxer said. "He sure as hell doesn't have any among his crew."

"I didn't think he would," Stark answered, coming out from behind the desk and leading the way to the door.

A few minutes later they were seated in the rear of Stark's limo, heading south on I-95.

"How long do you think my debriefing will take?" Boxer asked.

"Two, three days at the most," Stark answered, turning up the air conditioning. "Are you planning to go someplace."

"A holiday for Trish and me. I want to go where I can wash out some of the muck that's in me."

"Bad as all that?" Stark questioned.

"Worse," Boxer said. "The bastards weren't content to kill my men, they had to torture them too."

"Torture?"

"They impaled them," Boxer said, his voice cracking with emotion, "then they cut their pricks off and stuck them in their mouths."

"Bastards!" Stark growled.

"Some day," Boxer said, "I hope I meet the man who gave that order and some day soon, I'm going to find and kill Morell. He was one of their agents."

"He's also one of ours," Stark said.

"That doesn't matter to me," Boxer replied with unrestrained anger. "I want him dead."

Stark pressed a button on his armrest and a small bar came out of the back of the seat in front of them. "I could use a drink about now. What about you?"

"Yes," Boxer said.

Stark poured a jigger of vodka into one glass and a jigger of scotch into another glass. He added two ice cubes to each and handing the one with the vodka in it to Boxer, he said, "To your men, living and dead."

"Good men," Boxer said, after he drank.

"The very best," Stark commented; then he asked after De Vargas's family.

"They'll manage, but they'll never be the same. The Lieutenant was their shining light."

Stark finished his drink, poured another, and said, "This business with Bush is serious. He's on the other side of reality, his doctors say."

"I never cared much for him," Boxer admitted. "But he was a brave man and —"

"Even when he was in the hospital, the doctors didn't hold out much hope for him, though they did say that, with some of the newer drugs coming out, they might be able to stabilize him."

"It's a tough rap for his family."

"Did you know that they were originally farm people from Kansas?"

Boxer shook his head.

"There's a sister and brother. Both are older than him. The sister is a history professor at Georgetown and the brother is a senior physicist at the Brookhaven Atomic Laboratory. Neither of them, when contacted by Bush's doctors, were concerned and now that he has killed a man, I strongly suspect they will be even less concerned."

Boxer shook his head. "I'm sorry for the man; I truly am."

"He hates you and Cowly," Stark said. "The two of you are on his hit list."

"And what about Lowe?"

"He wants to make out with her, among other things he wants to do to her," Stark answered.

"He tried to, aboard the *Turtle*," Boxer said.

"So I gathered from your preliminary report," Stark told him. Then finishing his drink, he said, "There's something else I want you to know about Bush."

Boxer raised his eyebrows. "What?" he questioned.

"The FBI and our people are certain he had help."

"You mean —"

"That's exactly what I mean," Stark said. "And what makes it worse, we don't know why anyone would want him free or who that anyone might be."

Boxer gave a long low whistle. "That's scary as hell!"

"It's more than just 'scary'," Stark said, "it's damn terrifying, I'd say."

Boxer put his empty glass down on the bar. "It just doesn't make sense."

"Not yet. But I'm sure it will and, when it does, it will be even more terrifying," Stark said.

For several moments neither one spoke, then Boxer asked, "Just where are we going?"

Stark's face broke into a smile. "Don't ask questions. Just enjoy the ride."

"I'll try," Boxer answered.

The jangling sound of the phone tore away the fabric of sleep and dissolved the dream Trish was having into reality. She reached over to the night table for the phone.

"I wanted to hear your voice," Borodine said, before she could speak.

Completely awake now, Trish answered, "I'm glad you called."

"Do we meet again tonight?" Borodine asked.

"Jack is back," she said.

Borodine fell silent.

"Darling, we'll find a way," she said.

Borodine remained silent.

"He was here when I returned."

"Where is he now?"

"He had to go out," Trish said evasively, suddenly realizing that it might be a mistake to tell Borodine anything about Boxer.

Finally Borodine said in Russian, "I love you."

And she answered with the words he had taught her.

"When will I see you?" he asked.

"Soon."

"Tomorrow, in the afternoon?"

Trish hesitated.

"I need you," he told her. "I need to be with you, to make love to you."

"I'll try," Trish answered. She looked at the clock. It was 1230:05. "Call me at eleven tomorrow. If Jack answers, tell him that you're anxious to see him. He already knows you're here."

"I will phone at eleven," Borodine said; then in Russian, he added, "Goodbye, my lover."

"Goodbye, my darling," Trish answered. She continued to hold the phone to her ear until she heard the click on the other end; then sighing deeply, she puffed up the pillow and settled down in the bed again.

"We're here," Stark announced happily.

"Where's 'here?'" Boxer asked, looking out of the window at the flat open country, much of which was salt marsh. About an hour before, the driver had left I-95 and had headed east toward the coast on a secondary road. Now they were on a dirt road.

"There," Stark said, pointing ahead to where there was a small marina, with dock space for no more than a dozen boats, two gasoline pumps, some equipment for hauling boats out of the water and putting them back in. Some distance back from the marina, there was a large white house, complete with a screened porch and a garden in front.

Boxer turned to Stark. "I don't understand," he said.

"It's mine," Stark grinned.

"Yours?"

"I own it. Everything you see, except of course the visiting boats, I own. I even own the *Anita*, that Dutch double-ender, tied up at the end of the dock."

The driver brought the limo to a stop in front of the house and got out to open the door for Stark and then for Boxer.

Stark motioned to Boxer, "Come, I'll show you around," he said.

Boxer fell in alongside of him and they began to walk.

"The house is really a guesthouse for the people who tie up here and want to get away from their boat for a night, or however long they want to stay," Stark explained. "But I have a three-room suite on the second floor overlooking the marina."

"You surprise the hell out of me," Boxer said. "This is a side of you I never suspected existed."

Stark laughed. "Something for me when I retire," he said, gesturing toward the house and then toward the marina. "It's also some place for me to come to and get away from my daily routine."

"Who takes care of it when you're not around?" Boxer asked.

"A retired CPO and his wife," Stark said. "They live in the house we passed up the road a ways."

Boxer commented on how nice the garden looked.

"Grow vegetables in the back. I get tomatoes this big," Stark said, using his hands to show Boxer how large.

It took Stark the better part of an hour to show Boxer around the marina and house. He even took him aboard the *Anita* and proudly pointed out the galley and living space. "You could spend a few days on board her without having to tie up at night."

Boxer was impressed and told Stark as much.

"Now," Stark said, after they had entered the house, "you and I will sit down and have drinks and lunch on the porch. I have a cook here who's the best for miles around. You just sit down on the porch while I check on lunch. There's a bar cart out there."

"I'm on my way," Boxer said and a few moments later he was pouring a vodka for himself. Holding the glass in his hand, he opened the screen door and stepped outside. That Stark had even thought about owning a place like this would have surprised him, but that Stark actually did own it was almost unbelievable.

The screen door opened and Stark said, "Com' on in and sit down."

"I have to tell you," Boxer said, re-entering the porch, "that I'd never have figured you for something like this. After all, you were a fighter jockey."

Stark poured himself a drink. "Yeah, but I always had a love for the sea. And besides," he said, sitting down on a wicker chair opposite Boxer, "I saw this place and I liked it, so I bought it. The marina shows a good profit and, even if it didn't I could afford to keep it."

"Here's to your hideaway," Boxer said, raising his glass. "May you enjoy it for many, many years."

Stark raised his glass. "I'll drink to that." And then in a much lower voice, he said, "Eventually, Jack, it will be yours."

Boxer wasn't sure he had heard correctly.

"I don't have anyone else to leave it to," Stark said. "No children. No family at all."

"I have —"

"I know you have money," Stark said. "But this place is more than money. I like to think there's a part of me here."

Boxer didn't know how to respond.

"Besides," Stark said, "I loved your mother and, if she hadn't married your father, you might have been my son."

"That's almost a frightening thought," Boxer said with a grin.

"You're probably right," Stark agreed. "But I have to leave it to someone and you're that *some* one."

Boxer nodded. "I guess I am," he said.

Stark nodded. "Well, I'm glad that's settled." And he finished his drink.

"I hope you don't have any more surprises for me this afternoon," Boxer said. "Remember this was supposed to be a calm day for me."

"I promise nothing," Stark answered.

"That answer has two meanings," Boxer said.

Stark shrugged.

"Do you want to let the other shoe drop now," Boxer asked.

"It's about Morell," Stark said.

Boxer stood up and went to the screen. "I'm going to kill him and nothing you or Kinkade might say will stop me."

"That won't bring your men back," Stark said.

"No, but it will make sure he doesn't kill any more men."

"He might kill you," Stark offered.

"He might," Boxer said, facing Stark. "But then again he might not."

"You intend to have a good old Western shoot-out, don't you?"

Boxer went to the bar and poured more vodka into his glass. "No, nothing as dramatic as that. I'll just kill him."

"Kinkade says Morell was —"

"I don't give a damn what Kinkade says or doesn't say. Morell led us into a trap."

"At least speak to Kinkade about it."

"No," Boxer said. "No. Kinkade has nothing to say about this. I'm going to kill him. End of discussion. I don't want to talk about it any more."

Stark nodded. "That much I can see for myself," he said.

"I'm sorry," Boxer told him. "I didn't mean to growl at you. But —"

"No need to explain," Stark answered, holding up his hand. "No need at all."

Boxer sat down again. "What did you say we're going to have for lunch?" he asked.

"Soft-shell crabs, shrimps, and scallops."

"Sounds good to me," Boxer said.

"Wait until you taste it," Stark responded. "She mixes them all together, seasons them, and then adds white wine."

For a while neither of them spoke.

Boxer filled his pipe, tamped down the tobacco, lit it, and puffed furiously. The mention of Morell was enough to get him angry, let alone any suggestion that he abandon his desire to kill him.

"Oh, by the way," Stark said, "Miss Wheeler asked to be remembered to you."

Boxer nodded. "She's quite a lady."

"She thinks you're quite a man," Stark replied. "She said that if it wasn't for you there would have been many casualties when the plane went down."

"The credit goes to my men, who went into the water to save the other passengers."

"Not according to her. She's quite a fan of yours."

"She was too frightened to know what was happening," Boxer said. "But it's nice to have a fan."

"She asked me to remind you that she has papers for you to sign," Stark said.

"I haven't forgotten," Boxer answered. "But I need to spend some time with Trish. She's becoming impatient with me."

"Are you going to marry her?" Stark asked.

"I don't know," Boxer said. "I really don't know. I want to marry her, but she has reservations. I really don't know."

CHAPTER 8

Former Congressman William McElroy sat at the head of a long conference table. Directly behind him was a large picture window that framed a stand of birch and a small grass-covered hill on which two horses grazed. In front of him, on either side of the table, were six men. Each man was provided with a notepad, a pen, and a glass. In the center of the table was a large pitcher of ice water.

Some of the men at the table were Latin types, others were distinctly Anglo-Saxon looking. All of them were well dressed and wore gold watches and diamond rings on their pinkies.

"Well, gentlemen," McElroy said, "thank you for coming out to my farm this lovely summer day. I invite all of you to be my guests for dinner and I hope there will be time to show you around. This farm has been in my family —"

"Please, McElroy, let's get on with the business at hand," one of the older-looking members at the table said.

"In time, Senator, in time," McElroy answered. He looked at the faces round the table. Several of the men were international captains of industry. Two were admirals in the navy of a South American country. One was an air force general. And beside the senator, there was a member of the White House staff.

McElroy cleared his throat. "Within a month we will begin the second phase of our operation. As you gentlemen know, the *Tecumseh* is safely hidden in a Greenland fjord. She will soon be making her way south to rendezvous with the *Shark*. And the *Shark* will be ours within the month."

The men exchanged glances and one of them asked, "We still lack a captain. How can the boat be moved without a captain who knows her?"

"We have a captain, gentlemen," McElroy said with a smile. "We are fortunate to have a man who knows the *Shark* from first-hand experience."

"You can't mean —"

McElroy flushed. "I don't mean Captain Boxer. I mean the man who should have had command of the *Shark* from the very beginning." To ready himself for the hard part, McElroy took a sip of water.

"Cowly?" asked the man from the President's staff.

McElroy shook his head. "Captain Steven Bush," he said.

"Christ, that's the psycho —" the senator started to say.

"The killings were unfortunate," McElroy said. "The men happened to be in the wrong place at the wrong time, as the expression goes. But Captain Bush is now in our care and I can assure you he is as normal as any of us."

"Are you sure he'll be with us all the way?" one of the admirals asked.

"He is anxious to be part of our group. His interest and sympathies are a mirror image of our own."

"And you say he has first-hand experience with the *Shark*?" the other admiral asked.

"He actually commanded her for a short period of time and, during her last mission, he was aboard as an observer."

"What exactly is wrong with him?" one of the industrialists asked.

McElroy was waiting for that question and he attacked it with the frenzy of a predator going after food. "Captain Boxer is what's wrong with him. Boxer and his communist friends — Admiral Stark and, yes, my former father-in-law, Kinkade.

Communists all of them." He paused and took another sip of water. "Bush discovered what they are and, to silence him, they put him away."

"How did you manage to find out where he was?" the same man asked.

"I still have many friends in the various services," McElroy answered.

"Are we to understand that you arranged his escape?" the senator asked.

McElroy smiled. "I not only arranged it, as you put it, I also was the one who drove what, in certain circles, is referred to as the getaway car."

For several moments the men at the table spoke among themselves.

McElroy watched them. He was glad of the opportunity to remain silent. So far everything was fine, but there was always the danger that someone would ask a question that could not be answered.

"All right," the general of the air force said, "Bush is our man."

The others agreed.

"Just one more question," one of the other industrialists asked.

Though McElroy nodded, his stomach twisted into a knot.

"Will we have the opportunity to meet and question Captain Bush ourselves?" the man asked.

McElroy slowly allowed himself to relax. "No," he said confidently. "The man has been through a terrible ordeal, a living nightmare. He has come to regard me as his friend and, indeed, I am. He has agreed to do what has to be done. A month is all the time he has to rest. I would not have him subjected to questions from anyone in this group. And certainly he deserves better at our hands than he received at theirs."

Again there was a flurry of discussion among the men at the table. This time, McElroy did not wait until it had subsided and said, "For those of you who would like to meet Captain Bush, you will have the opportunity at dinner."

"Why isn't he here now?" the man on the President's staff asked.

"This is an executive planning session," McElroy answered. "The captain, though very important to our plan, is certainly not and never could be, part of this group. We gentlemen are the future rulers of the world."

"I certainly like the sound of that," the man said.

"Now to business," McElroy said. "I have information that the *Shark* will be moved from its present position to another berth where new and more sophisticated electronic gear will be installed. A tug will be used to accomplish the move and it will be made at night. That part has been arranged by friends of ours in the navy. Only four members of the crew will be aboard during the move and none of them will be officers. Before the tug gets underway, our men will board her and get rid of the crew. We will then move the *Shark* out into the main channel and head toward the ocean."

"What about the four men aboard the *Shark*?" another industrialist asked.

"They will have to be killed," McElroy answered.

"So will the crew of the tugboat?"

"Yes. Anyone who does not belong to our group will be killed," McElroy said. He took another sip before continuing. "The tug will bring the *Shark* to a rendezvous point with another vessel, where Captain Bush and several other members of the *Shark*'s crew will board her for the journey to rendezvous with the *Tecumseh*. The rest of the operation you know. I will be aboard the *Shark* for the entire operation. Are there any questions about this?"

"Is there a specific reason why you will be aboard the *Shark*?" the senator asked.

McElroy nodded. "Since this plan originated with me, I think it's my duty to be there. I will serve no purpose here."

"I'm satisfied," the man from the presidential staff said.

One by one the other men at the table indicated that they agreed to everything they had heard.

McElroy beamed at them and said, "The next time all of you hear from me I will be aboard the *Shark* and on my way to change the destiny of the world or mankind."

The men smiled back and the meeting was over.

"Those of you who intend to stay for dinner please feel free to wander around the farm. I will join you shortly but first I have a few things to take care of."

Out of the dozen men, only five remained for dinner.

McElroy excused himself and hurried to another room, where Bush was. "How are you?" he asked, opening the door.

Bush was sitting on the bed reading a *Newsweek*. "I have a slight headache."

"Here, take this," McElroy said, reaching into his pocket for a small bottle of pills. "Nothing but aspirin," he explained.

Bush left the bed, took the bottle from McElroy, and walked over to the dresser where there was a tray with a pitcher of ice water and a glass.

"I told our governing body that you will be joining us at dinner," McElroy said.

Bush swallowed the pill before he answered, "Good. I'd be happy to meet them."

"They might ask you questions about the *Shark* and Boxer."

Bush nodded. "No problem," he said, handing the bottle back to McElroy. "I'll tell them anything they want to know."

"I'm sure they'll be particularly interested in how the communists operated aboard the *Shark* and how they managed to get you committed to the hospital."

"I will tell them what they want to know," Bush said.

"Excellent!" McElroy exclaimed.

"Now I have a question for you," Bush said.

"Fire away."

"It concerns Cowly and Lowe," Bush said.

"Only a matter of another day or so," McElroy said. "It takes time to arrange to have someone killed and another person kidnapped."

"I can appreciate that, but we don't have too much time. According to your own timetable we'll be at sea within the month."

"I can only assure you that arrangements to do what you ask are going forward," McElroy said.

"I want Cynthia Lowe here, if you get my drift."

"She will be here."

"Did you know she was Boxer's whore?"

"Boxer has many whores," McElroy said bitterly. "Too many for any one man."

"Cynthia actually loved me but they forced her to have sex with Cowly," Bush said. "I'm sure she was drugged just as I was."

"I wouldn't doubt that for a minute," McElroy said.

"Once I have her here," Bush explained, "I'll make her understand just what has been done to her."

"And I'm sure she will," McElroy answered.

Bush smiled. "I'm sorry that I will not be able to see Boxer's face when he finds out that I had Cowly killed and that Cynthia is finally mine. That would be a sight worth seeing."

"I could have Boxer killed as well," McElroy offered.

Bush frowned and his face clouded. "That, sir, is not what God intended. God does not demand his death, only that he suffer for the rest of his life."

McElroy nodded. He understood Bush. He too had a mission to perform for God. But his mission demanded a blood sacrifice. He was chosen to rid the world of the whore of Babylon and then to cleanse the world of the communistic scourge. "We both have holy missions," he answered reverently.

Boxer rested in the rear of the limo. "I had a wonderful day," he said to Stark.

"That's good. The next few are going to be busy for you. I want you to go down to the yard and have a look at the *Shark*. There's additional electronic gear that's going to be installed: new equipment that will improve the UWIS and your sonar. And some scrambling gadgets to confuse the enemy's sonar."

"How long do you think I'll have to be in Washington?" Boxer asked.

"A week at the most. Better make that two."

"Then I want a month for myself and Trish."

"No problem," Stark said. "Any idea where you'll go?"

Boxer shrugged. "Anywhere she wants to. Some place where I can lose some of what I have in my head."

Stark remained silent.

"Losing De Vargas was a hard blow to take," Boxer explained. "In some ways he was a better officer and friend than Tom."

"You know, of course, he'll have to be replaced," Stark said.

"Wait until I come back from vacation."

"There's no hurry," Stark said. "No hurry at all."

Boxer fished out his pipe and tobacco pouch and carefully filled his pipe, then lit it.

"What about Rugger's son?" Stark asked.

"The boy is okay. He and John got on famously. I was thinking of finding a good boarding school down here — not a military school but one that has some discipline."

"I'd think twice about it before I got that involved," Stark said.

Boxer puffed on his pipe. "I won't do anything rash, but I think the boy can be something, if he has the chance."

"Are you sure you're not seeing what you'd like to see rather than what is really there?"

"Maybe a bit of both," Boxer admitted. "But if the kid has the stuff to become some kind of professional, I want to give him the opportunity."

"Just remember that you're not his father," Stark cautioned.

Boxer nodded. "I may not be his father, but I sure as hell can be his friend."

"Maybe," Stark answered.

"I guess I'll have to trust that 'maybe'," Boxer said, "and hope that he understands."

When Boxer arrived at the apartment, Trish told him that Borodine had phoned and had left a number where he could be reached.

Boxer immediately returned Borodine's call and as soon as the person on the other end spoke, he knew he was speaking to Borodine. "I want to see you tonight," Boxer said.

"Perhaps it is not convenient —"

"Comrade Captain Borodine — ah, I forgot, my CNO told you that you're an admiral now."

"And I have been told that you too have been promoted," Borodine said.

"We'll talk about it at dinner."

"Are you sure?"

"Hold on a minute," Boxer said and, putting his hand over the mouthpiece, he turned to Trish, who was standing nearby in front of the dresser mirror and brushing her hair. "You don't have any objections to meeting Borodine for dinner?"

"I don't mind it, but I think you'd be better off without me. After all," she said, "the two of you share things that I can never hope to understand."

"Nonsense. You'll find him an attractive, interesting man."

"If you really want me to, I'll go."

"Thanks," Boxer said and, removing his hand from the mouthpiece, he said, "Everything is set, except the time and the place."

"You tell me when and where and I will be there," Borodine answered.

"Hold on a minute," Boxer said and this time, when he spoke to Trish, he did not screen out the conversation. "Can you think of a really interesting restaurant?" he asked her.

"It depends on the kind of food you want," she answered.

Boxer said to Borodine, "Trish knows everything there is to know about this town."

Borodine chuckled.

"There's a very expensive French place that recently opened on Seventeenth and Q streets," Trish said. "It's called Chez Helena, but it already might be too late to get a reservation."

Boxer told Borodine the name of the restaurant and where it was located. "About twenty hundred would be a good time," he said.

"I will be there, Comrade Admiral Boxer," Borodine said and hung up.

Boxer broke the connection, then dialed information, and asked for the telephone number of the restaurant.

"Bet you don't get a table," Trish teased.

"How much? No, I have enough money. Make it what?"

"What do you want?" she asked, moving closer to him. She was wearing only a diaphanous white negligee.

Boxer was going to say, Anything you give me, but instead he put his arm around her waist and drew her to him.

A man with a French accent answered the phone.

"This is Admiral Boxer," Boxer said, "I would like a table for three at eight this evening."

"I am sorry, Admiral, there is nothing available until at least nine-thirty."

"That's too bad," Boxer said. "Admiral Duchamps —"

"Duchamps?" the man asked.

"He is here as the official naval —"

"Admiral, there is a table available," the man said. "I just miscounted the number of reservations for this evening."

"That will be for three at eight this evening," Boxer said.

"Certainly," the man answered.

Boxer thanked him and hung up.

"That was pure deception. It doesn't count," Trish said.

"I got the table, didn't I?" Boxer asked, lifting the back of her negligee and placing his hands on her buttocks.

"We never agreed to terms," Trish said. "You never told me what you wanted."

Boxer buried his face in the hollow of her stomach. She smelled of heather. "I want you," said. "I want you."

She caressed the top of his head. "Then take me," she answered in a whisper. "Take me, my love!"

Boxer stood up and slipped the negligee off her; then lifting her into his arms, he carried her to the bed and set her down on it. For several moments, he just stood and looked at her. She was not just a beautiful woman, she was an exquisitely beautiful woman. Her long blond hair accentuated her summer tan and somehow enhanced the features of her face.

She raised her arms to him. "Just don't stand there looking at me," she said.

"I enjoy looking at you," he answered, beginning to undress.

She laughed. "Now that's a revelation!"

"No," he said, getting into bed next to her, "It's the simple truth." And drawing her to him, he put his lips to hers and kissed her...

Trish wore a simple black cocktail dress with a décolleté neckline. She let her hair spill down over her shoulders.

Boxer was in civies.

They entered the restaurant at five minutes past eight. A young woman directed them to the maître d', who said, "Your table is ready, Admiral."

"We'll wait at the bar for the other member of our party," Boxer said.

"As you wish," the maître d' answered.

Boxer guided Trish to the bar. "Every man who saw you wishes he was me," he whispered, as they sat down.

"And every woman wishes she was me," Trish answered.

Boxer took hold of her hand and kissed the back of it. "What would you like to drink?" he asked.

"A very dry martini," she answered.

"This is posh," Boxer commented, looking around after he had ordered a Stoli on the rocks for himself and a martini for Trish. The walls were covered with dark, red velvet and the bar itself was teak, with an enormous mirror behind it.

Just as the barkeeper brought their drinks, Boxer spotted Borodine's reflection in the mirror. "Borodine is here," he told Trish. "The maître d' is telling him we're at the bar."

A moment later Borodine came toward them.

Boxer turned and stood up.

"Ah, Comrade," Borodine boomed, "it is a pleasure to see you."

"And for me to see you, Comrade Admiral," Boxer answered, aware that everyone at the bar was looking at them.

They embraced and kissed one another on the cheek, and then Boxer introduced Trish.

Borodine took hold of her hand. "You are more beautiful than your picture," he said, kissing her hand.

"Thank you," she answered. Then looking at Boxer, she said, "I never knew you showed my picture to anyone."

"Under most unusual conditions, I assure you, Comrade," Borodine said.

"I'd be most interested to hear about them," Trish answered.

"What would you like to drink, Comrade?" Boxer asked.

"I will start with vodka," Borodine answered. "But at the table we must drink champagne to celebrate our meeting."

"Done!" Boxer exclaimed and ordered a Stoli for Borodine.

With a drink in hand, Borodine toasted the men of the *Shark*.

Boxer returned the courtesy and toasted the crew of the *Sea Savage*.

Then Borodine looked at Trish and said, "To you, lovely lady, may you have much happiness and long life."

Trish flushed. "Thank you, Comrade," she said.

Each of them had another drink and most of their conversation consisted of small talk.

Eventually Trish suggested they go to the table.

"Good idea," Boxer said.

The three of them left the bar and the maître d' escorted them to the table and presented them with elaborately printed menus.

As soon as he departed, the sommelier, a white-haired individual with a very large key attached to a huge chain of gold around his neck, approached the table and, speaking English with a French accent, he asked, "Would you care to see a wine list, or would you prefer to have me recommend a wine that would complement your food?"

"Two bottles of the best champagne you have," Boxer said. "And a bottle of the best red and one of the best white wine in the house."

"Are you sure you don't want to look at the list?" the sommelier asked.

Boxer shook his head.

The man left the table.

"Now," Boxer said, "to make things easier, suppose we refer to one another by our first names."

"Good," Borodine said.

"Good," Trish seconded, imitating Borodine.

Boxer opened the menu and, realizing that everything was in French, had to admit that he was lost.

"I'll translate for you," Trish offered. Then, looking at Borodine, she asked, "Do you want me to do the same for you?"

"I can manage," he said.

Boxer decided to order a veal dish, Trish chose seafood, and Borodine said he would try the steak.

When the waiter came, Trish ordered for Boxer and herself. Then Borodine, speaking flawless French, proceeded to order for himself.

"I didn't know you spoke the language," Boxer said.

"French, German, and English," he said. "It's required for every officer who is promoted past the rank of lieutenant."

Boxer shook his head. "I'm lucky we don't have that requirement," he said. "I'd have never managed it."

"I was sorry to hear how many men you lost on your last mission," Borodine said.

Boxer looked at Trish.

"If you'd prefer me to leave —"

"No," Boxer said in a soft voice. "No. Igor knows how it feels to lose men." He looked across the table at his Russian counterpart. "All but six of the original strike force."

Borodine nodded.

"You probably know what they did with those they captured?" Boxer said.

"Yes. It was a horrible thing to do."

"Horrible to see," Boxer said.

"What did they do?" Trish asked.

Boxer took a deep breath and slowly exhaled.

"Better she does not know," Borodine said.

"I'm not a child!" Trish protested.

Boxer nodded and explained what had happened on the beach.

"Oh, my God," Trish exclaimed. "How could they do something like that to other men?"

"To them it is the ultimate insult," Borodine answered.

Trish put her hand on Boxer's arm. "You poor darling. I am really very sorry for you."

The sommelier returned with two assistants who carried the bottles of champagne and wine.

Boxer eased the conversation away from the events of his last mission to Borodine's stay in Washington.

"I love every minute of it," Borodine said. "You know I was assigned here before. I liked it then, but I like it much better now. And now I have more free time to do things."

"Trish, why don't you show Borodine some of the sights," Boxer said. "I'm sure you can take him places and show him things that he could never visit or see on his own."

"I have been many places and seen many things on my own," Borodine said. "But if your lovely lady can show me more, I would be grateful."

"What about it, Trish?" Boxer asked.

"Yes, I think it would be fun to show Igor the sights," she said. "There are places outside of Washington that are interesting too."

"If you will be my guide, I will be a dedicated tourist," Borodine said with a smile.

A waiter came to their table with the house salad, and dinner began.

"What really fascinates me," Trish said, spearing the filet of sole almondine, "is how the two of you can sit here talking as if you were the greatest of friends —"

"We are," Boxer said. "Aren't we friends, Igor?"

"Yes. But let us find out what it is that fascinates her?"

"It fascinates me that obviously you are great friends and yet sometime in the future each of you will try to kill the other."

"It fascinates us too," Igor answered with a smile and offered to pour more champagne for Boxer and Trish.

"None for me," Trish said.

"Pour," Boxer told him.

"It is how do you say here, our —"

"Duty," Trish offered.

"No, that would make it routine," Boxer said.

"I am not sure one word would explain it," Borodine commented.

"We are friends," Boxer said, "because we share so much. Our experiences are the same."

"Very much the same on many different levels," Borodine added.

Trish flushed.

"I think the wine has gotten to you," Boxer chided. "Will you look at the color of her cheeks?"

"If you gentlemen will excuse me," Trish said, "I think I'll put some cold water on my face."

Borodine started to stand.

"I can manage, thank you," she said.

He nodded and resumed his seat.

"Isn't Trish marvelous?" Boxer asked.

"Marvelous," Borodine answered, lifting his glass and finishing the champagne that was left in it. "Absolutely marvelous!"

The three of them were standing under the restaurant's awning. A light rain was falling and there was a chill in the air.

"Good night," Borodine said, kissing Boxer on both cheeks and then kissing Trish on her mouth. "Next time we have dinner together I will pay the check."

"You will pay," Boxer said. Then with a grin, he said, "I'm thoroughly swacked out."

"Swacked out?" Borodine questioned.

"Drunk," Trish said.

"Take him home and put him to bed," Borodine said. Then in a whisper he added, "I will call you."

Trish nodded.

"You better call me," Boxer said, "or I'll be angry at you."

Borodine nodded and walked off to the right.

"Hey, where are you going, Igor?" Boxer called after him.

Borodine smiled but did not answer. He turned the corner and headed directly toward the embassy car that was waiting for him.

The driver was slumped down behind the wheel, asleep.

Borodine rapped on the side window.

Startled, the driver bolted up. A few moments later, he was out of the car. "Comrade Admiral, I apologize for sleeping," the man said in Russian, as he opened the rear door.

"I would have done the same," Borodine answered, settling onto the seat.

"Back to your hotel?" the driver asked, slipping behind the wheel.

"Just drive," Borodine said.

"In the city?"

"Anywhere. Just drive," Borodine answered, sitting back and lighting a cigarette. Being with Boxer and Trish was nothing like he thought it would be. He had not realized how difficult it would be not to put his hands on her, not to look at her, and, worst of all, not to be able to spend the night with her.

Borodine touched a button and the window slid down. He knew that he could never marry Trish, but her sexuality enthralled him. She was like no other woman he had ever made love to. She thrilled him in ways he couldn't have imagined existed.

He blew smoke out of the window and asked himself what was he going to do. He understood the danger involved: danger from his own people, danger from the Americans. But he couldn't see himself giving up Trish, at least not yet.

Borodine stubbed out the cigarette and closed the window. He was just about to tell the driver to take him back to the hotel, when the man said to him, "Comrade Admiral, we are being followed."

"For how long?" Borodine asked.

"About ten minutes?"

"Are you sure?"

"Yes."

"Our people?" Borodine asked.

"I cannot tell."

"Are you armed?"

"Yes," the driver answered. "And there is also a weapon in the glove compartment.

"Hand the gun to me," Borodine said.

"No need to," the driver said, "the car just turned onto a side street."

Borodine lit another cigarette and let the smoke rush out of his nostrils.

"I enjoyed myself," Boxer said, lying down next to Trish. "I think Igor liked you."

Trish didn't answer.

"What did you think of him?" Boxer asked.

"He's a very attractive man," she said, "but not my type."

"It's good to be next to you, Trish," he said.

"It's good to me too," she answered. "The time that you're away isn't easy for me."

"Nothing is easy," Boxer responded sleepily. "Nothing."

Trish realized he had fallen asleep and had left her unsatisfied physically and emotionally. She wanted to talk about him and Igor. She wanted to discover something that would explain how these men could be friends — and they were certainly that — and still hunt one another. She understood nothing about that side of them. She knew each as a lover, nothing else.

Trish slipped out of bed and, putting on a light robe, padded into the living room where she lit a cigarette and dropped into a large club chair to think. For the present, she had no intention of giving up either man. Each of them filled her needs and, if what she gave of herself to them was a measure of her love, then she loved both with equal passion.

She got up, flicked the ash on the tip of her cigarette into an ashtray, and then went to the window overlooking the balcony. She knew that sometime within the next few days — perhaps when they were on vacation — Boxer would ask her to marry him and she would refuse, telling him that she wasn't yet ready to make that kind of a commitment. And she wasn't, not with Boxer or Borodine, should he ask, though she knew he wouldn't.

Trish moved away from the window and sat down in the chair again. That she was betraying Boxer hardly bothered her. If the years that she had been married to McElroy taught her anything, they taught her to take her physical pleasure where and when she could. Boxer couldn't expect her to go without sex whenever he was away. He couldn't expect her to deny herself pleasure just because he wasn't there to give it to her. Even if he did, her needs were much too powerful for her to live that way.

"Trish?"

Startled, she leaped to her feet and turned toward the door.

"Com'on back to bed," Boxer said.

"I thought you were asleep," she said, stubbing out her cigarette.

"Was. Then I realized you weren't there," he said.

She walked to where he was standing. "I just couldn't get to sleep," she explained. "And I was afraid I'd wake you if I tossed and turned."

Boxer put his arm around her and, as they walked back into the bedroom, he said, "I didn't tell you about my meeting with Stark."

"Tell me in the morning," she said, as they approached the bed. "Now you get in that bed and get some sleep. Tomorrow you begin your debriefing."

"Yeah, I know. I'm not looking forward to it," Boxer said, drawing the light cover up to his neck. "I'm not looking forward to it at all."

CHAPTER 9

The debriefing periods exhausted Boxer and made it impossible to forget the men he had seen on the beach. He became restless and irritable and, rather than inflict himself on Trish, he urged her to go places with her friends.

Boxer spent the afternoons, if the weather was nice, walking along the river or just walking the streets of the city. He was having difficulty coming to terms with what had happened on the last mission.

One afternoon, just before the onset of twilight, Boxer wandered over to the Lincoln Memorial and with several other people, all of whom were tourists, he stood looking up at the statue for several minutes. And he suddenly realized he was looking beyond the statue to the wall where the words of the Gettysburg Address were incised. When he came to the words "that these dead shall not have died in vain," he stopped and, with his vision blurring, he reread them intoning them to himself. Then, wiping his eyes with a handkerchief, Boxer clenched his teeth and silently vowed that he would make sure that his men had not died in vain either, that the people responsible for his men's agony would be called to account for what they had done. That evening he returned to the apartment feeling better than he had felt since he had returned.

On the fourth day of the debriefing, the session ended late in the morning. Boxer phoned Trish, hoping to spend the rest of the day with her, but she wasn't home. Disappointed, Boxer decided to go into Washington, have lunch, and then go to a travel agency to set up the vacation he and Trish were going to take as soon as the debriefing sessions were over.

By the time Boxer had left Langley, had driven back to Washington, and had parked in the Georgetown area, he was hungry. Other than a small luncheonette, which did not interest him at all, there wasn't any place to eat on the street where he was. He wanted to sit down at a table, have a drink and then a leisurely lunch. He stopped at the corner and looked up at the street signs. He was at the corner of Thirty-ninth and Beecher Streets, not too far from the Naval Observatory. Knowing there were several good restaurants in the immediate vicinity of the observatory, he was about to cross the street and walk toward it when a woman called out, "Captain Boxer. Captain Boxer. Please wait!"

He turned. Francine Wheeler had almost caught up to him.

"I'm so glad to see you," she said, offering her hand. "I was on my way to lunch and would have missed you."

Boxer shook her hand. "Missed you?" he asked, realizing how lovely she looked. She wore a simple white blouse and plaid skirt.

"You were on your way to my office, weren't you?"

Boxer let go of her hand. "To tell the truth, I was trying to find a restaurant —"

"I just assumed that —" she flushed. "That just proves that lawyers should not make assumptions in court or out of it."

"Not to worry," Boxer said, "I won't tell anyone that you assumed anything if you tell me where I might find a decent restaurant where I can relax and have lunch at the same time?"

She stared at him.

"Is anything wrong?" Boxer asked, feeling uncomfortable under the intense scrutiny of her green eyes.

"I have an idea," she said. "Why don't you come back to the office with me and I'll prepare lunch for the two of us and, while you're there, you can sign the papers that need your signature."

"But you were on your way to lunch," Boxer protested. "I don't want to stop —"

"You're not stopping or keeping me from anything. I just wanted to get out and be with people for a while."

"No special appointment?"

"None," Francine answered.

"Then I'd have to say," Boxer told her, "that your offer is the best I've had in a hell of a long time."

Linking her arm with his, she said, "But first we have to make a quick stop at the deli around the corner."

"I'm in your hands, Francine," Boxer said, as they started to walk.

"Trust me," she said. "You couldn't be in better hands."

Boxer didn't reply, but, for reasons he couldn't explain, he felt she was telling the truth.

The store was an old-fashioned German-type deli, the kind Boxer remembered having gone to when he was a boy. The man who ran it was short and fat and wore a clean white apron.

"My mother used to shop in a store like this," Boxer said. "It even smelled like this."

"We'll reminisce about our misspent youth later," Francine said. "Now let's choose what we'll have for lunch."

"You do the choosing," Boxer responded. "I'm much better at eating than picking."

Francine nodded, let go of his arm, and, stepping up to the counter, proceeded to order a number of delicious-looking salads. "What we don't eat, I'll finish off another time."

"Fine with me," Boxer answered, scanning the shelves of imported items. There was everything from tins of cookies to small glass jars of spices.

"Done," Francine announced.

Boxer turned. "Please, let me pay for it," he asked.

"No."

"Half?"

Francine shook her head. "I owe you," she answered. Then to the owner of the store, she said, "That man saved my life and the lives of several hundred other people."

Boxer felt the color rise in his cheeks.

"I pay," Francine said, "and you eat. That's our arrangement."

Boxer took the bag from her. "The least I can do is carry this," he said.

"I have no objection," she said.

Outside the store, Boxer asked if she had something to drink.

"A whole bar full," Francine answered, linking her arm with his.

A few minutes later, Boxer found himself standing on the steps of an old brownstone while Francine unlocked the door.

"The kitchen is upstairs," she told him, pointing to a flight of steps that was off to the left. "My office is down here but I have a six-room apartment upstairs and guest accommodations in the attic."

"How old is the house?" Boxer asked, walking up the steps.

"About a hundred and twenty, maybe a hundred and thirty years old."

Boxer gave a low whistle of appreciation. "One thing is for sure," he said, "the houses built today will never last that long."

Francine agreed.

Boxer set the bag down on the table and looked around. The kitchen was thoroughly modern and spotless.

"Go into the living room and pour yourself a drink," Francine said. "There's ice in the fridge. And in the cabinet over there, you'll find bar nuts and pretzels."

"What do you want to drink?" he asked.

"Same as you."

"I'm a vodka person."

"I'll have the same," she said.

Boxer walked into the living room. It was exquisitely furnished in a way that couldn't be labeled. There were huge cushions on the floor in front of a good-sized fireplace. Near the window was a concert grand piano. A tan-colored sectional sofa faced several large, comfortable-looking club chairs of the same color. A brick wall was partially covered with a beautiful Japanese tapestry of what, he was certain, had to be a picture of one of the Shinto shrines on the Inland Sea. And on every wall there were pictures. Some were paintings; others were photographs, both in color and in black and white.

"Lunch is almost ready," Francine called from the kitchen.

"Drinks are on their way," Boxer answered, going to the small bar in the far corner of the room. He poured two vodkas and walked back into the kitchen for the ice.

"Let's eat in the living room," she said, picking up the tray of food.

"Fine with me," Boxer responded, putting two cubes in each of the glasses and following Francine into the living room.

"I think we'll be better off on the cushions than anywhere else," she said.

"If I get too comfortable, I just might fall asleep," Boxer said.

Francine set the tray down on the carpet and took a moment to arrange two cushions. "That should do it just fine!"

Boxer hunkered down and settled against a large orange-colored cushion, leaving Francine with a light-blue one.

"This is crabmeat salad," she said, pointing to one plate. "Chicken salad in this one. Tuna here. The rest you can see for yourself."

Boxer picked up his drink. "To the lovely queen of the salads," he toasted, "and to a lovely lady who came to my rescue."

Francine blushed.

"Come, raise your glass," Boxer said.

They touched glasses, drank, and then began to eat.

"Really good," Boxer commented. "And it does bring back all sorts of memories."

"I was born and raised in the Midwood section of Brooklyn," Francine said, "so I really know what you're talking about."

"Where exactly is that?" Boxer asked, putting tuna salad on a small square of pumpernickel.

"The area around Midwood High School and Brooklyn College. My family lived in the yellow-brick apartment house directly across from Midwood High School. I used to shop for my mother at a German deli that was on Nostrand Avenue and Glenwood Road."

"The store I went to was on Fourth Avenue," Boxer said.

"So the two of us are from Brooklyn!" Francine exclaimed with a smile.

"To Brooklyn," Boxer toasted.

Francine clinked her glass against his. "I knew we had a lot in common," she said.

They continued to eat and exchange bits and pieces about their past until Francine decided it was time for Boxer to sign the papers.

"You don't have to go downstairs. I'll bring them up if I can get to my feet."

Boxer stood up and, taking hold of her hand, he easily lifted Francine to her feet, bringing her accidentally hard against him. "Sorry," he said.

She colored and backed away. "Couldn't be helped," she said in a choked whisper, turned, and headed for the steps.

Boxer added more vodka to their glasses and remained standing until Francine returned. "I refreshed our drinks," he told her.

"It wouldn't take much more for me to begin to see a parade of pink elephants," she said.

"The room is too small to hold more than one or two; three at the most," Boxer answered.

"Better sign these," she said, handing several sheets of paper to him. "Sign where it is marked with an X."

"And this is the end of the legal procedures?" Boxer asked, as he placed the papers on the top of an end table and began to sign them.

"Yes. You don't ever have to see me again," she answered.

Boxer stopped and, looking straight at her, he said, "I wouldn't like that. Besides, I want to retain you to handle my legal affairs. I can do that, can't I?"

"Yes, you can," Francine answered in a tremulous voice.

"Then consider yourself retained," Boxer said, putting his signature on the last piece of paper.

"I want to warn you my fees are high," Francine said.

"I'm a millionaire several times over. I can afford it," he said, handing the papers back to her.

"There is still some unfinished business," Francine told him.

"What?"

"The matter of the painting," she said.

"Would you believe, I completely forgot about it," he lied, wondering what her reaction would be.

"And several drawings: some in pen and ink, others in pastel."

"I take it that legally they belong to me?" Boxer asked.

Francine nodded.

"But you want them?" Boxer asked.

"Yes, I want them," she answered in a low voice. "I'll even buy them from you."

"May I see them?" Boxer asked.

"They're upstairs. One is in my bedroom and the others I have kept in a large portfolio," Francine explained, motioning to him to follow her.

"Mind if I take my drink along?" Boxer asked.

She shook her head and, walking out of the living room, she started up the narrow flight of steps.

Very much aware of the movement of her body, Boxer followed Francine.

"This way," she said, leading him into her bedroom. "The painting is on the far wall."

Boxer stopped in the doorway. The painting was hung over Francine's king-size bed. It was a large oil canvas of her nude. She was on her back. Her body was curved toward the view, her legs were drawn up, and her thighs were splayed. Her left hand covered her left breast and her right was partially draped over her love mound. Every detail of her body was shown. Her eyes were half-closed and there was an expression of ecstasy on her face. Except for the luminosity of the figure, the painting was dark, though after a while it became clear to Boxer that she was lying on some sort of divan.

"I'll bring the portfolio," Francine said.

Boxer nodded and drank part of the vodka. Now he understood why she wanted to keep the painting.

"Here are the drawings," Francine said. "There are only six of them." She put the portfolio on the bed, opened it, and spread the drawings over the bed.

Boxer moved to the foot of the bed and looked down. Two were done in ink and four in pastel. All of them were erotic drawings of Francine. He finished his drink and, looking at her, he said, "He must have loved you very much."

"There was never anything like that between us," she said.

"Then why —"

"Did I pose for him like that?" she asked.

Boxer nodded.

"About five years ago," she said, "I was in analysis. I had just been divorced and I wasn't at all sure of myself as a woman. Rugger was a client of mine and in a casual conversation he said that he would like to do a nude painting of me. These are the results. He captured a sexuality I never knew I had. In no small way he made me feel whole again."

Boxer looked at his empty glass and wished he had poured more vodka into it.

"Now you know why I want to keep them," she said.

"Yes," he answered, picking up one of the ink drawings that showed her on her knees with her rump toward the viewer. "I think you're wrong. I think Rugger did love you."

She flushed.

"But you didn't love him, is that it?" Boxer asked. Suddenly he was angry.

"I liked him. He was a good friend, but I could never feel toward him the way he felt toward me."

"Did he ask you to go to bed with him?"

"Why are you asking all these questions? Either I keep the drawings or you take them."

Boxer ran his hand over his beard.

"I don't understand why you've suddenly became angry at me," she said.

"Rugger was a good friend of mine," Boxer said.

"He must have been to leave you —"

"You don't understand — for Christ's sake, you don't understand. Do you know how he died?"

"An accident at sea," she said quietly.

"He was murdered," Boxer said harshly. "Shot in the back of the head and thrown overboard."

"Oh, my God!" Francine exclaimed. "Oh, my God."

Boxer turned away from her. He was trapped by his own feelings for her. Part of him wanted Rugger to have made love to her and part of him was glad that he didn't. Suddenly he realized Francine was at his side.

"Come," she said, taking hold of his arm. "Come and have another drink."

"I'm sorry," Boxer said. "I don't know why I became angry at you."

"Because you're full of anger and full of grief. It is not an easy combination to live with. Come, have another drink."

Boxer shook his head.

"Coffee then?"

"Yes, coffee," he said.

They walked down the steps. This time Boxer went first and Francine followed.

"The coffee will be ready in a few minutes," Francine said, starting for the kitchen.

Boxer reached out and taking hold of her arm, he stopped her. He fought down the impulse to take her in his arms and kiss her. "The painting and drawings are yours," he said.

She smiled at him. "You're a good man," she told him. "A very good man." She threw her arms around his neck and kissed him. "I've wanted to do that ever since you saved my life."

With a smile, Boxer said, "I won't tell you the things I'd like to do with you."

"No, don't tell me," she answered, her voice suddenly going to a whisper.

"Coffee," Boxer said. "Better make the coffee."

Boxer's debriefing ended the next afternoon and, before he left Langley, Kinkade called him into his office. It was the first time since Boxer's return that they met, but Boxer was certain that Kinkade had listened to the tapes of the debriefing sessions.

"I was told you wanted to see me," Boxer said, standing in front of Kinkade's desk.

Kinkade looked up from the paper he was reading. "I want to talk to you about a very sensitive matter."

Boxer remained silent.

"Please, sit down," Kinkade said, gesturing toward the chair at the right side of the desk.

Boxer sat down.

"There are actually two sensitive matters I want to discuss with you," Kinkade said.

"If Morell is one of them," Boxer told him, "you can save us both a lot of time and trouble. There is no room for discussion: I'm going to kill him."

Kinkade leaned back in his chair. "Morell is a professional. If push comes to shove, he'll kill you before you ever —"

"Listen, Kinkade," Boxer said harshly, "the only way you're going to stop me from killing him is to have one of your agents kill me. And if you do that, there are several other men who will pick up where I left off."

Kinkade uttered a weary sigh.

Boxer suddenly realized how old and tired the man looked.

"You're a hard man," Kinkade said, "a very hard man."

Boxer shrugged. He wasn't going to admit that he wasn't as hard as Kinkade thought he was: the last mission proved that. "What's the second sensitive matter you want to discuss?" Boxer asked.

"Trish, my granddaughter," Kinkade said.

Boxer stiffened. He and Kinkade had crossed swords over Trish on more than one occasion. But he sensed something in Kinkade's manner that dampened his belligerency.

"I'm concerned about her," Kinkade said.

Boxer raised his eyebrows questioningly. "Is something wrong that I don't know about?"

Kinkade waved the question aside. "Nothing physical," he said, "but I don't think she's happy."

Boxer leaned slightly forward. "I don't think so either," he said. "I think she's upset with me."

"Are you going to marry her?" Kinkade questioned.

Boxer pursed his lips. "I was planning to ask her when we were on vacation."

"What do you think her answer will be?"

"I don't know," Boxer said. "I really don't know. Since I returned, I sense that there is something different about her, something I can't put my finger on."

"The few times I've seen her, I felt that too. Are you sure everything between the two of you is all right?"

"Trish was angry at me for going to try and rescue Rugger and then — well she doesn't understand certain aspects of my life. But maybe in time —"

"She's a very spoiled woman," Kinkade said.

"I know that," Boxer admitted. "But we do have a very intense sexual relationship."

"I don't doubt that," Kinkade commented.

"I'm going to ask her to marry me when we're on vacation," Boxer told him again.

"And if she should refuse?"

"I don't see why she should," Boxer answered. "But if she does, then I think the two of us will have to do some hard thinking about our respective futures."

Kinkade nodded and then he said, "Thanks for being so honest with me about Trish. I appreciate it."

"I know she means a lot to you," Boxer said. "And she means a lot to me."

"Will the two of you be my guests for dinner tonight?" Kinkade asked.

"If you don't mind having dinner with us and a Russian," Boxer said with a smile.

"Admiral Borodine?"

"Yes."

Kinkade ran his hand over his chin. "I've always wanted to meet him," he said.

"You can tonight at the Riverside Restaurant."

"His people will not like the idea that he's dining with me," Kinkade said, "no more than I like the idea that the two of you are friends."

"He may refuse when he finds out that you'll be there," Boxer suggested. "After all, he's not a fool."

"All right," Kinkade exclaimed, "I'm willing if he is!"

It was nine when McElroy entered the Riverside Restaurant and took a place at the bar that allowed him to see everyone who entered or left the establishment. Because he had been informed by his contacts in the Navy Department that Boxer had returned, McElroy had spent the last five nights visiting Trish's favorite restaurants. There were only a half-dozen places where she really enjoyed dining and he knew that if he were persistent, he would see her.

McElroy looked at himself in the mirror behind the bar and was satisfied that even his close associates would not recognize him, so perfect was his disguise. He had a gray goatee, a gray wig, and horn-rimmed glasses. Each night he wore a different disguise. He even rented a different car to drive from restaurant to restaurant. And for each restaurant, he had worked out several different escape routes and committed them to memory. To get out of the Riverside, he would make for the kitchen, then out a side door, up an alleyway that opened onto the street. By that time, he would have gotten rid of his disguise and be close enough to his car to be able to get in it and drive off. He was counting on the confusion to help him to get away.

He caught the barkeeper's eye.

"What will it be?" the man asked.

"Wild Turkey and branch water," he answered. The barkeeper poured the bourbon into a shot glass. "Mix them?" he asked.

McElroy nodded and when the drink was mixed, he picked up the glass and was about to drink when he saw Trish, Boxer, and Borodine enter the restaurant. His heart skipped a beat and then began to race and his hands trembled. It took a few moments for him to regain his composure and, when he did, he picked up the glass and drank. Now all he had to do was chose the right moment to act. That he was in total command of the situation gave him an enormous feeling of exhilaration and power. When he saw Kinkade enter the restaurant, McElroy took it as a sign that God had chosen him to be His instrument, otherwise why would He put all his enemies in one place at the same time? Even Bush, who had his own agreement with the Almighty, couldn't deny it.

McElroy finished his drink and ordered another. He drank it as slowly as he had the first. Then he left the bar and walked into the men's room. He went into a stall, closed the door and latched it. He took the .22 automatic he'd been carrying out of his pocket, eased a round into its chamber and, clicking off the safety, he slipped the gun back into his right pocket. A few moments later, he was back at the bar, and he paid for his drinks, and put two dollars down for the barkeeper. Then he stood, turned, and, certain that God was at his side, started to walk into the restaurant area.

Trish was happy. She was with the three most important men in her life; two were her lovers and the third was her grandfather.

"Igor," Boxer was saying, "you must come with Trish and me to the country. I know a special place that you'd like."

Borodine nodded vigorously.

"You never told me that you knew of a special place," Trish said laughingly.

"Oh, I do," Boxer responded.

"Tell me!"

"If I don't know about it," Kinkade said, joining the conversation, "then it probably doesn't exist."

Trish laughed. She could tell that, in spite of the fact that he was a Russian and that he was her secret lover, her grandfather liked Borodine. If he hadn't, he would have remained silent as a clam for the entire evening.

"If my friend says he has a special place," Borodine said, "then I believe him."

Boxer pointed his finger at Kinkade. "I'll take you there."

"I don't go to a place unless I know where it is," Kinkade answered.

"Good answer, Grandpa," Trish said, picking up her glass of water. "Neither do I."

"Neither do you what?" Borodine asked.

Trish saw the man with the goatee while she was drinking. He was coming toward the table. She started to lower her glass. There was something familiar about the man. Something — "Oh no!" she exclaimed and threw herself in front of Boxer. The next instant an explosion of pain filled her skull.

Boxer, Borodine, and Kinkade spent the rest of the night pacing back and forth in the hospital waiting room. Their clothing was stained with Trish's blood and each of them said nothing to the others.

At exactly 0530, according to the digital clock on the wall of the room, the weary-looking surgeon entered. "I'm sorry," he said gently, "but Miss Kinkade will never regain consciousness. The brain was badly damaged."

"Brain dead?" Boxer forced himself to ask.

The doctor nodded. "Yes."

Kinkade sobbed.

Boxer put his arm around the old man and, looking at the surgeon thanked him.

"I wish the news was better," the doctor responded, turned, and walked out of the room.

"Let's get out of here," Boxer said, leading Kinkade toward the door. "Let's get out of here and go somewhere. Anywhere but here!"

Igor nodded.

CHAPTER 10

Bush was in the pilothouse of the *Restless Lady*, a commercial tug that was tied up at a pier on the James River. It took exactly two minutes for him and four other men to overcome and kill the tug's crew and take command of the boat. No one even heard the three short bursts of machine-gun fire.

"Carter, make sure the bodies are weighted," Bush said. "I don't want them coming to the surface for a while."

"Captain, they'll stay down for a month of Sundays," Carter answered, leaving the pilothouse.

Bush switched on the shortwave radio and dialed the harbor master's frequency. "The tug *Restless Lady* calling the navy harbor master."

"Go ahead, *Restless Lady*," the navy operator said.

"Request permission to enter security zone... ETA zero three hundred... Clearance number five six zero dash four two one."

"Stand by."

"Standing by," Bush answered, switching off the hand-held mike.

Carter returned. "Our engineer said that the engines are old but in good working order," he said.

Bush didn't answer. Carter was his EXO. The three other men were technical specialists: one for the sonar and radar equipment, one for engineering, and one for fire control.

"*Restless Lady*," the navy operator said, "you're cleared to enter the security zone."

"Roger that," Bush answered with a smile. He switched off the radio and said, "Let's get under way, Mr. Carter, we have a rendezvous with fate."

"Yes, sir," Carter answered, saluting smartly.

Lashed to the *Restless Lady*, the *Shark* was slowly eased away from its berth. Bush was at the helm. He would have liked to make a dash for the open sea, but he was waiting for the fog before he did and, according to the last-minute weather information given to him by McElroy, that fog was due to roll in about 0400.

Carter came into the pilothouse. "Six men aboard the *Shark*. The only officer is the DO and he's up on the sail playing captain. All the others are rates. They're below in various parts of the boat."

"Use the gas grenades," Bush said.

"What about the DO?" Carter asked.

"Any way you have to," Bush answered, "but I want him off that bridge as quickly as possible."

"Aye, aye, Captain," Carter said, saluting.

Bush took one hand off the helm and returned the salute. He was going to run the *Shark* the way it was meant to be run: by the book, by strict standards.

Carter switched the radar on. "Fog," he said. "Dead ahead. Range two thousand yards."

"Roger that," Bush answered. "Board the *Shark* and take out the crew."

"Yes, sir," Carter said, saluting again.

Bush repeated the courtesy and then rang the engine room for more speed.

Less than fifteen minutes later, the *Restless Lady* moved the *Shark* into the dense fog. Carter left the pilothouse.

Bush switched on the radio and listened to the transmission between the ships in the bay and the harbor master. The fog was causing every ship to slow down to a snail's pace. Moving the *Shark* out under cover of the fog was part of the plan. In fact, the entire operation had been moved up by several days because a huge storm was brewing in the South Atlantic, which forecasters were predicting would turn into a late-season hurricane. The worse the weather, the better it would be for the mission.

Carter returned, a gas mask slung over his shoulder. "All of the *Shark*'s crew are dead," he reported, "and their bodies have been dropped over the side."

"Well done," Bush replied.

"Venting is now taking place. It should be completed in ten minutes."

"Ready the rest of the crew to go aboard the *Shark* in fifteen minutes," Bush said. "Make sure the *Restless Lady* continues on course."

"Everything has been checked. She'll head straight for the dock and with the explosives aboard her, she'll blow it and everything for a hundred yards around her out of the water."

"That should cause enough confusion to keep the navy busy for a while," Bush said. "We'll dive as soon as we cut the *Shark* free."

Carter looked at his watch. "Ten minutes," he said.

"Ten minutes, Mr. Carter," Bush answered, licking his lips.

Suddenly the radio came alive. "*Restless Lady*, this is Security... Do you read me?"

"Security, this is the *Restless Lady*... I read you loud and clear," Bush answered.

"You're off course... Check your heading."

"Roger that," Bush answered. "Stand by for heading check." And switching off the mike, he turned to Carter. "Board the *Shark* now."

"Aye, aye, sir," Carter answered.

Bush switched on the mike. "Heading reads seven two degrees," Bush said.

"Negative," the voice said. "You're six five degrees… Correct to seven two degrees."

Bush smiled and eased the helm down a bit. "Correcting," he answered. "Sorry about that."

"Roger," Security answered. "Keep a sharp lookout tonight… The fog is very dense around the shoreline."

"It's dense out here too," Bush answered.

"Out," the voice said.

Bush switched off the mike and secured the helm, left the pilothouse and leaped aboard the *Shark*. "Stand by to cut forward and aft lines," he called out.

"Standing by," two of the men answered.

"Cut lines!" Bush answered.

Within moments two axes severed the thick lines that bound the *Shark* to the *Restless Lady*. The *Shark* fell back. "Everyone below," Bush ordered, as he himself entered the sail and hurried to the COMCOMP.

Bush made the SYSCHECK. All systems were green. He pressed a button and the bridge began to sink into its well. Then he switched on the MC. "This is Captain Bush," he said. "All hands stand by to dive… All hands stand by to dive." He hit the klaxon twice; then keying the EO, he said, "Give me full power."

"Moving to full power," the EO answered.

Bush dialed in fifty feet into the AUTODIVSYS and set the bow planes to five degrees. The sound of escaping air filled the

Shark. Bush watched the instruments. The boat was submerging. His eyes went to the depth gauge above the COMCOMP. The needle was almost at the fifty-foot level. He switched on the UWIS and scanned the bottom some forty feet below. A green light began to flash on the COMCOMP and a bell sounded. The dive was complete. He activated the AUTONAVSYS and, putting in his present position, he dialed in the latitude and longitude where he would rendezvous with *Corsair*, the ocean-going yacht that was carrying not only the rest of his crew and McElroy, but also Cynthia Lowe. Bush looked forward to spending time with her and there would be time for that before he met up with the *Tecumseh*. He wanted her at his side when he took his rightful place as one of the chiefs of the New World Government.

Harbor Security watched the blip on the radar-scope for two minutes before he tried to raise the *Restless Lady* again. She was coming toward the dock too fast.

He made two attempts to call her before he turned to the DO and said, "I have a developing red here."

The DO immediately pressed a button that put everyone on yellow alert.

"The *Restless Lady* is not responding to my radio call... She's heading straight for pier number twenty-one with the *Shark* in tow."

"Range?" the DO asked.

"Two thousand yards."

"Speed?"

"Eight knots."

"Try the emergency frequency," the DO said.

"I did... No response."

The DO checked his own scope and bit his lower lip; then, making his decision, he pressed the red-alert button. A klaxon began to blare and, switching on the base PA, he said, "All hands on pier twenty-one... All hands on pier twenty-one, evacuate... All hands, evacuate pier twenty-one... All hands, evacuate pier twenty-one."

The explosion sent a burst of flames over two-hundred feet high and shattered every window in a radius of five hundred yards. The fire raced along the pier, consuming it in a matter of minutes, and then spread to the piers on either side of it.

It was hours before the fire was brought under control and Stark and a special team of investigating officers could get close enough to the burned-out hulk of the *Restless Lady* and discover that the *Shark* wasn't there.

A grim-faced Stark walked into Kinkade's office and slammed the door.

"Just what the hell happened?" Kinkade stormed. He was haggard-looking and there was pain in his eyes. "How could a civilian tug get the job of moving the *Shark*? My God, man, where are we now?"

Stark slammed a briefcase down on Kinkade's desk. "Shut up, Kinkade," he growled. "I've just been raked over the coals by the President and every damn member of the cabinet. I don't want any bull from you."

"You're lucky they don't crucify you in public," Kinkade said.

"There are people in both our departments that made it possible for the *Shark* to be hijacked, but we'll deal with that later. Right now we've got things to occupy ourselves with. First, a possible sighting of the *Tecumseh* came in a few hours ago."

"From where?"

"North. Greenland. She's heading south. My guess is that she's going to rendezvous with the *Shark*."

Kinkade leaned forward. "Why?"

"You'll know why when you've listened to this tape. It also explains why the police haven't come up with any leads about who shot Trish."

"What has she to do with this business?"

"Listen," Stark said, taking a portable tape recorder out of his briefcase and switching it on.

"Mr. President, this is William McElroy," the voice on the tape said, "I and my colleagues have engineered the hijacking of the *Tecumseh* and the *Shark*. We will do what you have not the guts to do. We will make a preemptive strike against the Soviet Union. By doing this we know that you will be forced to make follow-up strikes. These attacks will neutralize the Soviets and let us get on with the work of creating what God has ordained should be on earth. I am nothing more than the instrument of God…"

"Christ!" Kinkade exploded.

"There's more," Stark said.

"Now to other matters. This message is for Admiral Stark and Mr. Kinkade. Admiral, Captain Bush is commanding the *Shark* and, as you know, he is an excellent officer who has been undermined by you and other communist naval officers. All of you will be tried for treason when the new government of the United States comes into being…"

There was another pause before McElroy said, "Kinkade, Trish had to be destroyed. She was the new whore of Babylon. I shot her. She will whore no more."

Shaken, Kinkade looked up at Stark. "The man's mad," he said in a tight voice.

Stark stopped the tape. "Mad and dangerous. The voice on this tape matches the tape made of the voice coming from the *Restless Lady*."

"Does Boxer know any of this yet?" Kinkade asked.

Stark shook his head. "We threw a news blackout over the fire and anything about the *Shark* is top secret. I know he has been at the hospital every day since the shooting. He and Cowly will be picked up some time today and brought to my office."

"Has the President notified the Russians?"

"Not yet, but he will."

Kinkade uttered a weary sigh and said to Stark, "Better sit down. You look as terrible as I feel."

"Worse," Stark said, dropping into the chair next to Kinkade's desk. "The President has ordered Boxer to command the attack submarine *Neptune*. The *Neptune*'s captain will be under Boxer's authority, but she's the fastest attack sub in port and we're directing the four other attack subs cruising in the North Atlantic to come under Boxer's command. Our allies have been asked to close off all choke points between here and the Arctic."

"We still have the Russians to worry about."

Kinkade nodded. "The chief feels that they'll understand the situation and join in the hunt for the *Shark*."

"And if they don't?"

"We'll have World War Three," Stark said in his gravelly voice. "But the truth is we need the Russians to help us and that's the way the chief is going to put it to them."

"The Russians are always hard to predict; they might decide to go to war," Kinkade said.

"The President knows that," Stark answered. "He's put the armed forces on a yellow alert. Everything is ready to go. All our missiles, all of SAC's bombers are airborne. He's going to tell them all this and ask for an immediate answer. If it comes to war, it might well mean the end of all of us."

For several moments neither man spoke. Then Kinkade said, "I need a drink. What about you?"

Stark nodded and he said, "I was sorry to hear about Trish."

"Thanks," Kinkade answered. "Thanks." He got up and walked to the bar across the room. "Scotch?" he called.

"That will be fine," Stark said.

"Ice?"

"Neat and make it a double shot," Stark told him.

Kinkade returned to the desk with two glasses, and handing one of them to Stark, he sat down. "Both men were her lovers," he said wearily.

"Both —"

"Boxer and Borodine," Kinkade said. "Boxer didn't know."

"Did McElroy?"

Kinkade nodded. "My guess is he did. Theirs was a marriage in name only. But enough of my personal problems. Enough." And raising his glass, he said, "To luck. We're going to need it."

"To luck," Stark seconded.

"And to Boxer," Kinkade said.

"To Boxer," Stark echoed.

Two hundred and fifty miles east of Norfolk, there was a ripple in the Atlantic. The ripple became a white seam as a periscope pierced the surface and made a three-hundred-and-sixty-degree sweep and fixed on the yacht *Corsair*.

"She's in place," Bush said to Carter. "And the weather is dirty. She's rolling." He pressed the control button and the periscope slid back into its well.

At the COMCOMP, Bush keyed the COMMO. "Exchange recognition signals with the *Corsair.*"

"Aye, aye, sir," the COMMO answered.

Bush did a SYSCHECK. All systems were green.

The COMMO keyed Bush. "Sir, signal recognition is positive."

"Roger that," Bush answered. Then switching on the MC, he said, "All hands, now hear this... All hands, now hear this... We're surfacing... We're surfacing." He hit the klaxon button once and set the AUTODIVSYS to zero. Then he keyed the EO. "Go to zero six knots."

"Going to zero six knots," the EO responded.

Bush touched another control button that elevated the sail. Then turning to Carter, he said, "Get the crew on board first. Then the woman and finally McElroy."

"Captain, McElroy isn't going to like that," Carter said.

Bush glared at him. "I gave you my orders," he said angrily.

"Yes, sir," Carter answered.

The instant the *Shark* broke water, the green indication light on the COMCOMP began to flash.

"I'll take the CONN topside," Bush said. "If the sea is too rough, we'll make the transfer by small boat. I don't want to risk damaging the *Shark.*"

Carter nodded.

Bush left the COMCOMP and hurried up to the topside bridge. The wind was blowing at fifteen knots and the waves were five to six feet high.

Bush keyed Carter. "We'll make the transfer by small boat," he said.

"Aye, aye, sir," Carter answered.

Bush keyed the COMMO. "Patch me through to the *Corsair,*" he said.

After a few moments the COMMO responded, "Patch completed."

"Captain, here are your orders," Bush said. "All of your people will be brought to the *Shark* in your lifeboats… The operation should take no more than fifteen minutes."

"Bush, this is McElroy, you bring the *Shark* alongside and get us the hell off —"

"Negative… I cannot risk damage to the *Shark*… Send Miss Lowe with the first boatload… Out." Bush put the mike down and keyed the EO. "Slow to fourteen hundred rpms," he said.

"Slowing to fourteen hundred rpms," the EO said.

Bush remained on the bridge until the transfer of his crew was completed; then he left the topside bridge and immediately looked among the fourteen newcomers for Cynthia. Many of the men were from South American countries and several looked as if they had come from various places in Europe, but he didn't see Lowe.

"Bush," McElroy said.

Bush turned. McElroy was standing off to one side. He was wet and looked angry. "*Captain* Bush," Bush snapped.

"Captain Bush, I want to speak to you," McElroy said.

"In a few moments, Mr. McElroy," Bush answered. Then, to Carter, he said, "Show the crew their quarters and then direct them to their duty stations."

"Aye, aye, sir," Carter answered, saluting.

Bush returned the salute; then, sitting down at the COMCOMP, he keyed the EO. "Go to twenty knots."

"Going to twenty knots."

Bush switched on the MC. "All hands, now hear this… Now hear this… Prepare to dive… Prepare to drive." He pressed the klaxon button twice and set a depth of one hundred feet into the AUTODIVSYS. Then he turned to McElroy. "Where's Lowe?"

"It was impossible to get close to her," McElroy said.

"Not good enough," Bush said. "I wanted her."

"I did everything possible —"

"We'll settle this another time," Bush said tightly. "Another time. Now leave the bridge and —"

"What do you mean 'leave the bridge'?"

Bush turned away and scanned the instruments on the COMCOMP.

Five days later the SO picked up a target and relayed its bearing, range, speed, and course to Bush.

"Can you ID it?" Bush asked.

"ID is the *Tecumseh*," the SO answered.

Bush smiled. Everything was going according to schedule. He keyed the COMMO. "Radio the *Tecumseh*; tell her we're close by; then patch me into the system… I want to speak to the captain… Use code eight and set the scrambler to position zero five."

"Aye, aye, sir," the COMMO answered.

Within a half-hour, Bush brought the *Shark* directly under the *Tecumseh* and expertly maneuvered her into the huge opening on the underside of the ship. The rough sea on the surface made the operation extremely dangerous, but Bush made it seem routine.

As soon as the *Shark* was safely inside the *Tecumseh*, the bottom door swung closed. And with a roar the giant pumps began to discharge the water from the holding bay. As soon as the water level dropped, below the level of the *Shark*'s deck, arc lights came on.

Moments after the lights made the bay as bright as day, the *Shark*'s forward hatch was thrown open and Bush scrambled onto the deck. McElroy followed.

Despite the heavy roll of the *Tecumseh*, Bush hurried along the catwalks. But the movement of the ship was too much for McElroy. He was forced to stop and, leaning over the rail, he vomited into the rapidly dropping water in the bay area.

Bush glanced disdainfully over his shoulder, then proceeded to the bridge of the supership to pay his compliments to Captain Trazado, who had engineered the theft of the *Tecumseh* and had expertly evaded detection.

The storm that had been developing for days was now a full-fledged hurricane and was named Delilah by the National Weather Service.

Two hundred feet below Delilah's fury, Boxer, Cowly, and Riggs studied the charts of the North Atlantic.

"We can't be too far behind the *Shark*," Boxer said. "But there's no way of knowing whether she's already met the *Tecumseh*, or if that rendezvous is still to take place."

"No new reports on the *Tecumseh*," Riggs said. He was a tall, lean man with a pirate-like mustache and graying black hair. "This weather doesn't make recon easy."

Boxer and Cowly sipped their coffee.

"They might decide to follow the hurricane," Boxer said, putting down his mug. "So let's try to guess where they are if they are doing that."

Riggs pointed to a satellite photo and said, "This is one big storm. The *Tecumseh* had the chance to pick her cover. She'd probably try to stay to the north or northeast of the storm."

"Depending on where she was headed," Cowly said. "Anyone care to guess where?"

Boxer picked his pipe up from the table and jabbed the pipestem at the map in front of them. "Three obvious routes if she intends to release the *Shark* to penetrate the northernmost waters of the Soviet Union. And that's the only way the *Shark*'s missiles will strike the heart of Russia."

"The Baffin Bay route is out," Cowly said. "The Kennedy Channel is too narrow for even the *Shark* to slip through undetected, let alone the *Tecumseh*."

"The only other choice for the *Shark*, whether or not she's in the *Tecumseh*'s belly, is east or west of Iceland," Riggs said.

Boxer nodded. "You've got it. That's what she'll try, unless they try to sneak between the Faroes and the UK."

"The Norwegians and Brits ought to have that sewed up pretty well," Cowly said. "But we can't discount the possibility they might try it. Neither can we discount the possibility that they might take a more roundabout route, though they probably wouldn't."

"In any case, they'll probably follow the hurricane if it veers east or west of Iceland," Boxer said; then he asked for the latest weather report.

Riggs keyed the COMMO. "What's the latest weather report?" he asked, listened for several moments, then said, "Roger that." Turning to Boxer and Cowly, he shook his head. "Delilah's heading dead on for Iceland."

"Christ," Cowly exclaimed, "if the *Tecumseh* is inside of her, we won't know her course until she comes out from under Delilah's skirts!"

"That's the way it looks," Boxer answered. "We'll keep on the same course and hold our depth."

Riggs nodded.

"This isn't going to be the easiest wait," Cowly commented.

"No wait is easy," Boxer responded; then he filled his pipe and lit it. He was thinking of his recent wait at the hospital, while Trish was in surgery. During the long night, he saw his future with Trish slowly dissolve. He had intended to ask her to marry him while they were on vacation, only to be told there would be no marriage. He blew a cloud of smoke toward the ceiling. When Stark and Kinkade told him that he had to put to sea again, he had told them he wasn't sure he could handle it. They had assured him he could.

"If you can't," Stark had said, "no one else can."

And Kinkade had added, "You know what we're up against better than anyone else."

"Skipper, are you all right?" Cowly asked.

Boxer nodded. "Only thinking," he explained.

CHAPTER 11

McElroy stared glassily into the hurricane through a spinning glass disk set into the window on the *Tecumseh*'s bridge. The disk was the naval equivalent of windshield wipers. Its rapid rotation threw off water for a clear view.

The view was unsettling to McElroy's stomach. Through the dim gray haze, he caught glimpses of the horizon standing at an unsettling angle. The horizon quickly dropped back to where it should be, then overshot.

McElroy, queasy since the stolen supership had entered the storm, could take no more. He vomited against the glass. The noisome liquid reeked of gin — an old salt's remedy that had failed to calm his stomach though it had certain other benefits.

"Clean it up," Bush said firmly. He was standing some distance from McElroy.

Captain Trazado, who was next to the helmsman, turned his attention to McElroy. "Clean it up," he said. "There's no one here to do it for you."

McElroy knelt and dabbed ineffectually at the mess with a handkerchief and then staggered to a chair bolted to the deck. He clutched the armrest and watched his vomit creep along the deck as the ship pitched. *Stupid bastards. They'll be the first to go*, he silently swore. *If Trazado had anything on the ball, he wouldn't have been booted out by his betters after the Falklands debacle of '82. And Bush sucking up to the Argentinian like one dog sniffing another.*

But neither Bush nor Trazado noticed him.

Trazado and the helmsman were looking through the spinning glass window into the guts of the storm.

Boxer looked blackly into his mug of coffee. "I've been drinking too much of this," he muttered.

"Me too," Cowly said.

The two of them sipped at their mugs. They were in the *Neptune*'s electronic warfare room looking at a group of intent young men bent over glowing screens in the dimly lit room.

Riggs handed the latest computer printout to Boxer. It was a map of the North Atlantic. "These dots are all the known ships. These circles are unidentified ships. The data comes from various sources. But nothing remotely resembles the *Tecumseh*."

"The numbers next to the marks?"

"Tonnage known or estimated."

"You're right," Cowly said, "Nothing remotely resembles the *Tecumseh*."

"We're still getting updates," Riggs said.

"Sure. But I think Murphy's Law is operating here," Boxer answered. "The *Tecumseh* isn't going to be spotted. Once the *Shark* gets past the Arctic Circle everything is going to become more complicated. We're going to stop looking for the *Tecumseh* and figure out how to find and kill the *Shark*."

"But —" Riggs started to protest.

"Stow it," Boxer snapped. "Assemble the five smartest men you have on board — officers and enlisted men. I want the smartest you have. Maybe they'll come up with something."

The COMMO keyed Boxer. "Message for you, Admiral," the man said.

"Read it," Boxer said.

"Russians to command search-and-destroy operations… Only the *Neptune* will join up with Russian forces… More information will follow… Igor Borodine is in command of Russian force. Continue on present course… Stark."

"Roger that," Boxer said and, turning to Riggs and Cowly, he related the gist of the message.

Cowly let out a long, low whistle.

"Thank God, the Russians believe us," he said.

"And thank God," Cowly added, "that Borodine is in command."

"Amen to that!" Boxer answered.

Just as the five men entered the officers' mess, Boxer took a bite out of a ham-and-cheese sandwich, which he swallowed quickly. "Sit down," he said. "We don't have much time to waste, so I'll get to the point. I want you men to try to figure out how to stop the *Shark* and the *Tecumseh*. You have no further duties. All the computers are at your disposal. Either I or Mr. Cowly will answer any questions you might have about either the *Tecumseh* or the *Shark*.

"Input codes for all computers, COMCOMP, CIC, and so forth," one of the young men said. "We'll need operational frequencies for all radars and sonars."

One of the officers answered. "We'll try to break into the computer systems of the two vessels using sensor input to reach the computer processors. If we can do that, they'll be under our control."

Boxer's brow wrinkled. "Maybe the COMCOMP won't let you get away with it."

"Just give us the codes and the control signatures," a lieutenant said, "and we'll do the rest."

Suddenly general quarters sounded and Rigg's voice came over the MC. "Battle stations... All hands to battle stations... Battle stations!"

The five men scrambled out of the mess area.

Boxer and Cowly walked quickly to the bridge, taking care to stay out of the way of the crew darting through the narrow passageways.

As soon as Boxer reached the bridge, he nodded at Riggs. "You're in command," he said.

Riggs nodded and turned his attention to the COMCOMP.

The SO keyed Riggs. "Target bearing one five degrees, range ten thousand yards and closing… Speed three five knots."

"Roger that," Riggs answered. Then to the helmsman, he said, "Come to course one six degrees."

"Coming to course one six degrees," the helmsman responded.

"Activate ECM… Let's see the screen," Riggs said.

"ECM activated," said a voice from the speaker.

A large monitor on the bulkhead was activated. The oncoming target was shown in perspective and grid. Speed, azimuth, and depth were displayed on the side of the screen.

"Torpedo —" Riggs began.

The image on the monitor split in two. Then four. Then eight.

Boxer couldn't count the number of multiple images that were on the screen. The ping sounds also increased.

Riggs keyed the FCO. "They're spoofing us… Activate AUTOWEPSYS… Fire when ready."

Boxer exchanged glances with Cowly. They might be facing only one torpedo, or a wall of them. Or none. They were actually facing one or more MAGPLATs — weapons that use various means to escape detection, including hiding under thermal layers, or regions of different salinity. They are built with materials that give them a low sonar detectability.

"Blue-laser intermittent fire," the FCO said.

The blue laser penetrated ocean water and was effective against some targets, but its range was relatively short.

"Target encountered," the FCO said. "Data updating in progress."

On the screen most of the multiple targets vanished. The confusing chorus of pinging diminished. A counter at the bottom of the screen couldn't make up its electronic mind whether one, two, or three torpedoes were approaching. At this range the laser could only act as a detector, not a weapon.

Riggs keyed the forward torpedo room. "Arm and load torpedoes. Program MAGPLAT target co-ords."

The TO acknowledged the order.

"Stand by to fire torpedo one."

"Standing by," the TO said.

"Approaching torpedo now in laser lethal zone," FCO reported. A few tense moments passed. "Target not responding," the FCO reported. "Will rescan."

"It must be a spook!" Boxer exclaimed. By now he had realized they had been spoofed by a ghost torpedo. And the MAGPLAT location had only a thirty percent chance of either one really being there. The MAGPLAT had fooled the *Neptune*'s battle computers into fighting phantoms.

"Full scan," Riggs ordered.

"Computers updating attack data," the FCO said.

"Arm EM SUBROC," Riggs ordered.

"Arming EM SUBROC," the TO responded and, after a few moments, reported, "Ready and armed."

Riggs keyed the FCO. "Feed scatter probability into SUBROC computer."

"Data being fed… Feeding completed," the FCO said.

"Fire EM SUBROC," Riggs ordered.

A dull thump passed through the *Neptune* as the submarine rocket was launched through the torpedo tube. If the EM, an electromagnetic warfare weapon, landed in the right place, it would jam the MAGPLATs' signals.

They watched the SUBROC's progress on the monitor. It reached the surface and left the water, climbing on an arc of fire into the hurricane. It fought to maintain control; its small electronic brain constantly changing the position of its air fins. Twenty miles away it nosed down and plunged back into the ocean and became a torpedo and began to hunt for its target. Suddenly it emitted an intense burst of electromagnetic energy triggered by a chemical explosion. The explosion did not harm their target. But the electromagnetic radiation burned out the MAGPLAT hovering in the sea nearby.

Suddenly the SO reported a cluster of three torpedoes.

They came up on the screen.

The pinging grew louder as the torpedoes homed in on the *Neptune*.

"Crash-dive!" Riggs shouted over the MC and at the same time pressed the klaxon control button three times.

Boxer and Cowly grabbed whatever support they could.

The *Neptune* plunged.

The sonar pings came faster and faster until they became one continuous sound.

The torpedoes went off the monitor.

Suddenly there were three explosions above them. The *Neptune* dropped as if pushed down by some huge hand.

Riggs keyed the DCO. "Report damage," he said.

"The sail took a proximity blast... Not a direct hit... Periscope and radar damaged... Some leaking... Nothing serious."

"Roger that," Riggs said and then asked the FCO for a full scan report.

"Probable MAGPLAT three zero one degrees... Reliability eighty-nine percent."

"Forward TO, lock on coordinates," Riggs ordered.

"Locked on coordinates," the TO responded.

Riggs ordered, "Fire torpedo one."

"One away," the TO said.

Boxer watched the TIC, the target indication clock.

Two-and-a-half minutes passed before the sound of the explosion rolled over the *Neptune*.

"Target destroyed," the FCO said. "Continuing full scan."

Boxer took a deep breath and exhaled slowly.

"Cancel crash dive," Riggs said over the MC. He keyed the DO. "Make two zero zero feet."

"Making two zero zero feet," the DO answered.

Riggs told the helmsman to come to course, "one five degrees."

"Coming to course one five degrees," the helmsman said.

Boxer waited a few moments; then he walked over to Riggs and, looking up at the blank monitor, he said, "Well done, Captain. Well done."

"Thank you, Admiral," Riggs answered with a smile.

As soon as the *Neptune* reached its cruising depth, Cowly radioed Stark for a complete set of the *Shark*'s input codes. Because the codes were top secret Stark required a detailed explanation as to why they were needed. It took several messages to clarify the matter and within a matter of hours, Cowly had the codes. Then he and Boxer met with the five members of the *Neptune*'s crew who were going to use them to break into the control computers of the *Shark* and the

Bush was seated at the *Tecumseh*'s FC console. Around him were grouped several of the ship's officers, his own EXO, Carter, and McElroy.

"The target has evaded your weapons," one of the men said.

Bush glared angrily. "It was only a demonstration. The boat was damaged, perhaps seriously. It is not worth our time to finish it off. In any case, it doesn't know our location."

"We should get on to more important matters," McElroy said. "We can't hide in this hurricane forever. Too many ships are looking for us. There are too many submarines ahead and behind."

"This demonstration was an important matter," Bush said, glowering at McElroy. "I was not playing games." He turned on his heel and left all of them standing in front of the glowing instruments.

A few minutes later Bush was walking along the corridor leading to the submarine bay. Midway between hatches, he paused and looked quickly over his shoulder. No one there. Strange. He had heard a voice and the voice was talking about him. "It's McElroy," he whispered. "And the bastard is plotting against me. But I'll win. I'll win."

Bush continued on, glancing back again at the sound of McElroy's laugh. He quickened his pace. His eyes were bright, stoked by the inner fire of fury. He'd show all of them. Not only would he attack the communists, the enemies of mankind, but he'd also destroy his enemies, Stark, Kinkade, Boxer, and now Lowe. He couldn't let another man possess her. He'd destroy the people who had betrayed him!

Bush paused to catch his breath. He felt as if he had just jogged five miles. Was it time for another pill already? He searched his pockets for the small plastic pillbox but couldn't find it. "Damn it!" he exclaimed. "I'll go back to my cabin later and get them. Now I have work to do." He straightened up and continued toward the submarine bay.

A short time later Bush was on the bridge of the *Shark*. He sat down in front of the COMCOMP and keyed the proper words. The heading MISSILE TARGETS came up on the missile firing screen and was immediately followed by a list of twenty Russian cities. Using coordinates from the NAVCOMP, Bush changed nineteen of the cities previously targeted to those that would be in the range of the *Shark* when she reached the Russian Arctic. But the twentieth city gave him pause; then with an affirmative nod, he quickly typed in Washington, D.C., and entered the exact latitude and longitude of the White House. From now on the inertial navigation system would keep those targets in the FC computer's brain no matter where the *Shark* was, whether she was inside the *Tecumseh* or not. Bush cleared the computer screen and returned it to a stand-by condition. He left the *Shark* and, making sure he was unobserved, left the bay area.

On a big screen in a room deep under the Pentagon, Hurricane Delilah continued her relentless crawl toward Iceland, veering slightly to the east.

"There's no magic answer, Kinkade," Stark said. "As long as she's covered by that storm, it's not going to be easy to find her and, when we do, we'll have another kind of trouble on our hands."

"Worry about that after we find it," Kinkade snapped.

"You're right," Stark answered, to Kinkade's obvious surprise; then he added, "that's why we're going to drop some of our best operatives into the storm. They'll try to make contact with the *Tecumseh*."

"What are you talking about? Frogmen?"

Stark shook his head. "Not frogmen. Dolphins."

Kinkade's eyebrows went up. "You're sending dolphins against what you yourself tell me is the world's most advanced weapon system."

"We've been using them for decades. They don't get much publicity and that's the way we want it. They protected our ships anchored in Vietnam harbors during the seventies —"

"Protected?"

"They were trained to kill Charlie's frogmen with a special lance fitted into their noses. But the dolphins we will be dropping into Delilah are retrieval specialists. They've located sunken ships, satellites that fell into the sea, lost torpedoes, that kind of thing. Now they've been told to locate ships the size and shape of the *Tecumseh*."

"You talk to them?"

"I don't, but the bio-techs do — in dolphin language, of course, that was synthesized by computers. And you know, we've found they share certain opinions with us."

Kinkade fell for it. "They do?"

"Uh-huh," Stark responded. "They don't like civilians telling them their business."

Kinkade scowled and turned his eyes to the storm on the screen.

Boxer and Cowly's second meeting with the team of five again took place in the officers' mess area.

"We'll try to enter the *Shark*'s computers by sending the entry code to her passive sonar," the young rate said, whom the other men called DB. "The guys are modifying our active sonar to do just that."

"If all goes well," another tech said, "no one aboard will know they've been penetrated, unless they constantly monitor the system. We'll be making authorized entry with the proper codes, so it won't signal the alarm."

"What if they changed their passwords?" Cowly asked.

"They probably have, if they're smart," the DB said. "There are several passwords for the different computers, as you know. If they haven't changed every single one, we can enter the computers whose passwords haven't been changed. From there we can enter the system."

"If you try the wrong password, COMCOMP will sound the unauthorized entry alarm," Boxer said. "How can you stop that from happening?"

"We can't. We're counting on the fact that since there were so few raiders involved, only one or two understand the *Shark*'s computer system. If we're lucky, they won't be anywhere near the COMCOMP when we try to enter the system."

Boxer nodded gravely. "All right, do it. Proceed slowly. If you get command of the *Shark*, destroy it." Boxer cleared his throat. The words sounded strange; they even had a strange taste to them. He cleared his throat again. "Do it any way you can. Make it quick and clean."

"Aye, aye, Admiral," the DB answered.

For the next twenty-four hours, it was a quiet time for Boxer. A time for him to think and grieve about Trish. But he knew that grief lasted only a short time and, when it finally passed, the person that was grieved for became part of a memory — sometimes sad, sometimes happy, often bittersweet. But always there.

Boxer was on the bridge, waiting for the latest hurricane report, when he was finally able to come to terms with what had happened to Trish and to acknowledge the fact that, if he survived this mission, he still had a life of his own to live.

"Delilah is heading east," Riggs said, looking at Boxer. "That means the *Tecumseh* will be following her and sailing east of Iceland. That's if she's still using the storm for cover."

"I would if I were in command," Boxer answered.

Riggs ordered the helmsman to change course.

The COMMO keyed Riggs. "Have a message coming in on sub-to-sub channel for you, Captain."

"Patch it through," Riggs answered.

"Calling *Neptune*... *Novgorod* to *Neptune*... Reply." The accent of the operator was distinctly Eastern European.

"*Neptune* to *Novgorod*, Captain Riggs here... Continue message."

"Admiral Borodine," said another heavily accented voice, "presents his compliments to Captain Riggs and requests permission to speak with Admiral Boxer."

Riggs frowned slightly. "Borodine?"

Boxer smiled. "He's a good friend." Then, taking another mike hooked into the MC, he said, "Boxer here."

"Hello, Comrade... How are you?" Borodine asked

"Well and yourself?"

"Well but sad," Borodine answered.

"Yes, I am well but sad too," Boxer said.

There was a moment's pause before Borodine said, "In eight hours we will arrive at the Iceland–Faroe Strait. If the *Neptune* turns east, you can rendezvous with us there."

"We've already turned east."

"Good… The *Novgorod* is leading a group of six attack submarines… If we fail to stop the *Tecumseh* in the strait, we will proceed to Soviet Arctic waters and sink her and the *Shark* there."

"The *Neptune* is leading several American submarines in an attempt to —"

"Your boat is the only one that will be allowed to join our force," Borodine said. "You understand I do not make such decisions. But I ask you to join us."

"Give me a moment to answer," Boxer said and switched off the mike.

"You can't do that," Riggs said.

"Captain, I hope you will not object if I exercise my special authority now."

Riggs's jaw muscles tightened. "As a loyal American officer, I cannot object, but personally —"

"I understand," Boxer said. "I really do." And switching on the MC, he said, "Comrade, please give me the rendezvous coordinates."

"I look forward to working with you," Borodine said, after he gave Boxer the rendezvous point.

"And I with you," Boxer said and he switched off the mike. "I know it's difficult for you to understand," he said to Riggs, "but Borodine and I are very good friends."

"Friends? Hasn't he tried his best to destroy you and the *Shark*?"

"Just as I have tried to destroy him and the *Sea Savage*."

"Once we're alone and surrounded by the wolf pack, we'll be helpless," Riggs complained.

Boxer did not want to discuss the matter. "I don't intend to take over your boat's operations, Captain. Not now anyhow. Please resume your station," Boxer said.

Riggs cleared his throat. "Your pleasure, Captain."

"My pleasure, Captain, has nothing to do with it," Boxer answered.

Stony-faced, Riggs turned to the helmsman and gave him a heading.

Officially he was known as dolphin five-oh-four. But its trainers called him Happy. A hundred feet below the North Atlantic, Happy swam and sent out high-frequency signals, which rebounded off objects that informed him of their presence.

Happy's natural sonar had so far not located any object the size and shape of the *Tecumseh*.

Every now and then, he'd surface, breathe, look around at the turbulent sea and then dive again into the calm depths. He worked his way north, following the program he had been given by his trainers just before he had been dropped by parachute ahead of the storm. His instructions were to swim toward the *Tecumseh* if he spotted it. But so far no *Tecumseh*.

Borodine and Viktor, his EXO aboard the *Sea Savage*, looked over the shoulder of a sonar operator at the display of a computer analysis of the echoes being tracked by the boat's passive sonar.

"It might be the *Tecumseh*?" Viktor suggested.

Borodine nodded and on the sub-to-sub channel, he keyed the *Stanovaya*.

"Proceed with message," the *Stanovaya* answered.

"Investigate target at two eight five degrees, range twenty-five-thousand yards. Use extreme caution. ID and report back immediately."

"Understood," the *Stanovaya*'s captain answered.

Borodine and Viktor walked back to the bridge. Aboard the *Novgorod*, Borodine was also its operational captain.

"Do you think we have a chance against the *Tecumseh*?" Viktor asked in a whisper.

Borodine shrugged. "We must try."

"We must try," Viktor echoed.

"Order battle stations," Borodine said in a matter-of-fact tone.

Viktor sounded general quarters and over the MC, he said, "All hands to battle stations… All hands to battle stations."

Borodine listened to the reports from the various section chiefs.

There was a tenseness in the boat that had a feeling all its own.

Borodine and Viktor continually scanned the readings on the COMCOMP.

Suddenly the COMMO keyed Borodine. "Message from the *Stanovaya*'s captain."

"Patch it through," Borodine said.

"Comrade Admiral," the *Stanovaya*'s captain said, "the target appears to be the *Tecumseh*."

"Return to formation," Borodine ordered; then turning to Viktor, he said, "have our COMCOMP do all the work. We'll control the attack from here."

"Aye, aye," Viktor answered and immediately went about the task of making the COMCOMP aboard the *Novgorod* the attack center, while Borodine issued orders to the captains of the other submarines to circle the *Tecumseh*.

"You must stay out of the range of her weapons," Borodine cautioned on the sub-to-sub channel. "Give yourselves a one-zero-mile radius between your boat and the target."

Borodine ordered the forward torpedo officer to arm the nuclear torpedoes.

On each submarine of the wolf pack the captain gave the same order, but the *Novgorod*'s COMCOMP would direct and launch the attack.

"All submarines attention," Borodine said. "All TOs stand by." He watched the instruments on the COMCOMP, waiting for them to show the optimum moment for firing. The digits came up on the attack grid. "Torpedoes away!" he ordered; then added, "All captains confirm."

One by one the captains reported that their torpedoes had been launched.

Borodine and Viktor watched the attack grid as the torpedoes homed in on the target. Moments after the launch, there was a series of coughing sounds from above as the killer darts left their deck modules. Each of the submarines launched their killer darts at exactly the same moment.

Borodine nodded. There would be a short wait now until all of the weapons reached their target, arriving almost simultaneously. Borodine hoped to overload the *Tecumseh*'s defensive system.

"I hope it works," Viktor said, half to himself.

"It's in the lap of the gods now," Borodine said, wryly since he was an atheist.

Bush, Trazado, McElroy, and several other men, who were leaders in the plot to control the world, were at dinner. The conversation between them was mainly political, with McElroy leading it.

Suddenly a klaxon sounded and from the intercom came a synthesized electronic voice of the computer. "Attention, battle stations… We are under attack… Battle stations."

Bush was out of his seat. He turned to Captain Trazado, and said "Leave the ship under computer control and come with me to the CIC. The rest of you can watch the battle on the monitors or in the CIC."

"Let's continue as we were," McElroy said.

But no one listened to him. They gathered around the monitors.

Reluctantly McElroy joined them.

In the dim light of the CIC, Bush and Trazado saw the attack strategy at a glance. A series of screens showed the attacking torpedoes and killer darts.

The ship's sensors could not by themselves see everything that was on the screen. Some of the images were being transmitted by MAGPLATs and hovering sonar buoys.

Even as Bush and Trazado watched, the nuclear torpedoes began vanishing from the screen. Symbols coming up on the screen indicated that various MAGPLATs were automatically detonating the torpedoes before they came anywhere near the *Tecumseh*.

The killer darts were decoyed into striking other MAGPLATs.

"The attack is over," Bush said triumphantly. He touched several buttons and the screen changed. The *Tecumseh* was a green dot in the center and around it were six flashing red dots. Bush ID'd them: all of them were Class Two, Victor Attack submarines. "The best they have," he said, pointing to the specks on the screen. Then, shifting his eyes to the ring of red dots, he added, "They're closing in; they'll try again. And by now they have notified other search teams of our position."

"Perhaps it is time to leave in the *Shark*," Trazado said. "A submarine will be faster and safer."

"No," Bush said. "There's more danger below than on the surface. We'll stick it out a while longer."

"But look at the map. By the time we get to Iceland, Russia's whole northern fleet will be waiting for us. In the *Shark* we might have a chance —"

"Don't tell me my business," Bush snapped. "I'm in command of this mission."

Trazado's eyes narrowed. "This is not the kind of decision that only one man should make."

"How *dare* you question me!" Bush shouted.

Trazado stood silent.

"We are not going to Iceland," Bush said heatedly. "Here's where the *Tecumseh* is going." And he jabbed his finger at a spot on the map.

"There?" asked Trazado, astounded. "Why?"

"You'll see," Bush answered. "You'll see and so will the rest of the world." Then he turned to the console and spoke into the voice control. "Lock on displayed targets," he said.

"Locked on targets," the computer's voice answered.

"Activate ASW system," Bush said.

"ASW system activated," the computer answered.

"Destroy targets," Bush said; then he calmly turned to Trazado and blew the top of his head off with a .45.

CHAPTER 12

"Target bearing one zero degrees... Range five thousand yards... Speed three five knots," reported the SO of the *Novgorod*.

"Come to course one five degrees," Borodine told the helmsman.

"Target three three degrees," the SO reported. "Target five zero degrees... Target two five degrees."

Borodine studied the scope. A curtain of homing torpedoes was heading for the boat.

The other boats began to report torpedo attacks.

"It could be another spoof attack," Viktor suggested, looking at the scope over Borodine's shoulder.

"I doubt it," Borodine answered. "Link computers for target sorting."

Once again the COMCOMP aboard the *Novgorod* was in command.

After a few seconds sonar screens on all the submarines displayed the positions of all the torpedoes that the COMCOMP aboard the *Novgorod* evaluated as being real. They were fewer in number than the previous display had shown.

"Coordinate killer dart attack," Borodine said. "Fire!"

The thumping sound of dart clusters being launched quickly followed.

"Probably MAGPLATs detected," the SO reported. "Forty percent probability."

"Coordinate attack on probable MAGPLATs," Borodine said over the sub-to-sub channel.

"Admiral, we've lost contact with the other boats," the COMMO reported. "Jamming."

"The MAGPLATs!" he exclaimed and shook his head. Without communication with the other submarines, it was impossible to make a coordinated attack. And without coordinated action to detect and destroy the MAGPLATs, they were lost.

"Captain, I've lost contact with the *Novgorod*," the COMMO reported to Riggs. "MAGPLATs are jamming their transmission."

Riggs checked the monitors. The passive sonar was also jammed. "Admiral, the Russians are in trouble."

"They're sitting ducks," Boxer said, "if they can't communicate with each other."

"Could be worse," Riggs said, "they could be fighting the *Tecumseh* itself."

Boxer glared at him but said nothing. Then he suddenly turned to Cowly, "Get the DB up here on the double."

It took less than two minutes for the DB to arrive, "Reporting as ordered," he said to Boxer.

Boxer outlined Borodine's problem; then he said, "I want to communicate in Morse code with him. Can you work with the SO and rig some sort of key to activate the sonar?"

"No problem, sir. Sounds primitive, but it should work."

"Good," Boxer said. "Borodine will be getting some acoustic and electronic spoofing from the MAGPLATs. But we're too far away to be affected. They can't talk to us, but we can warn them of approaching targets."

"What if their SO doesn't speak English?" Cowly asked.

"I'd bet that he does," Boxer answered. "And if he doesn't, Borodine does. We don't have a problem there."

"Do you think your friend would do the same thing for us, if the situation was reversed?" Riggs asked.

"I like to think so," Boxer answered; then he added, "I'm sure he would."

Borodine made several attempts to contact the other submarines and failed. He made the decision to turn and run and was just about to order a change of course when the SO keyed him.

"Comrade Admiral, there are strange signals coming in on the passive sonar... They are almost like code."

Borodine switched on the speaker.

"International Morse code," Viktor said. "It's Boxer... He says he'll try to help... He says he'll spot targets for us since he suspects we're being spoofed."

Borodine grinned.

"More coming," Viktor said. "He says that he will take over command of our search group."

"What?" Borodine asked.

"And," Viktor said, "it is now up to us to go along with his plan."

"Glad he leaves us some authority," Borodine muttered.

"More," Viktor said. "Since this is only a one-way communication setup, there can be no consultation. He will transmit a list of targets and coordinates visible to his detection systems. He is assuming that since the *Neptune* is out of spoofing range these will be real targets."

Borodine agreed.

By code Boxer proceeded to direct the Russian submarines' fire. When the *Novgorod*'s turn came, Boxer recommended they destroy two of the nine torpedoes heading for them.

"Fire torpedoes one and two," Borodine ordered.

"Torpedoes one and two away," the TO confirmed as the homing torpedoes picked their targets and sped toward them.

"Rearm tubes," Borodine ordered.

"Rearming," the TO answered.

"Helmsman, come to course two five degrees," Borodine ordered.

"Coming to course two five degrees," the helmsman repeated.

Long moments later, the distant explosions echoed through the submarine's hull.

"Real targets destroyed," the SO confirmed. "Three phantom targets off the screen."

"Boxer was right on the mark," Viktor said.

"Admiral, the *Pervoz* is gone," the SO reported.

The sound of another explosion rolled over the *Novgorod*.

"I can hear the hull breaking up," the SO said.

"Crash-dive!" Borodine shouted. "Crash-dive." He struck the klaxon control three times. He keyed the EO. "Full speed."

The bow of the *Novgorod* tilted sharply downward. The vessel plunged into the depths of an undersea canyon.

"The torpedoes will follow us," Viktor said, "no matter how deep we dive."

"Not if we can find a thermal boundary, or another saline region," Borodine answered.

"The *Takhtoyamsk* is gone," the SO reported.

Borodine watched the depth gauge. They were two thousand feet down. He couldn't dive much further without rupturing the submarine's outer skin. He keyed the DO. "Level off," he ordered.

"Leveling off," the DO answered.

"Screen clear of targets," the SO reported.

Borodine nodded. They had obviously gone through a thermal boundary or a saline layer.

"Message coming from the *Neptune*," Victor said. "Confirms that two of our group have been destroyed. And — and the *Tecumseh* has been sighted by a spy satellite a hundred miles from the Faroes... All available forces are being turned toward her."

Borodine immediately adjusted several dials on the COMCOMP to calculate the quickest course to the Faroes. "Come to course one five degrees," he told the helmsman; then keying the EO, he said, "Go to flank speed."

"Going to flank speed," the EO answered.

"Boxer says we'll rendezvous at the Faroes," Viktor said.

"Tell him," Borodine answered, "I look forward to it."

Sweating, McElroy was lying in his bunk. He wondered why he suddenly felt better. He lay there, sensing the room around him. He slowly began to realize he was in the crew's quarters. Why? He sat up. The deck wasn't pitching. They must have left the hurricane. Good. Now he could stop gulping those damn seasickness pills.

He heard someone coming, looked toward the door, and saw Bush in his captain's uniform, buttons all polished and his shoes shiny as black glass. McElroy felt rumpled and at a disadvantage.

"Come with me, Congressman," Bush said.

"Come where?"

"Never mind where."

"We're out of the storm, aren't we? And doesn't that put us in danger of being spotted?"

"We've been spotted, just as I planned we would. Get up."

"Now just a —"

Bush slipped his hand out of the jacket pocket. "This is a .45," he said. "Now, move!"

McElroy stood. "Have you gone completely mad?"

Bush ignored the question. "Exit into the corridor and walk aft, Congressman," Bush said. "I don't really need your help for this, but I wanted someone to see what the result of our mission will be. No one deserves that honor more than you."

"Where are the others?" McElroy asked.

"Already locked in their tomb," Bush answered, "though it will be a while before they are dead."

"Where are we going?" McElroy asked again.

"Have you ever been aboard a submarine, Congressman?"

"The *Shark*!" McElroy exclaimed.

"She's like no other boat ever built," Bush said, "and she was given to a man who never loved her as I did. They gave Boxer the *Shark* and you, you gave Cowly Cynthia. Don't think you fooled me. You never intended to give her to me."

"I did. I swear I did."

They reached the bay and McElroy stopped.

Bush jammed the .45 into his back. "Walk or you're a dead man."

McElroy crossed over from the catwalk to the deck of the *Shark*. Within moments, he was inside the steel hull and then on the bridge.

"Sit there," Bush said, "while I get the *Shark* out of the *Tecumseh* and under way. You make one unnecessary move and I'll shoot your kneecaps off."

"I won't move," McElroy answered in a terrified voice.

At 0800 a P-36 Orion of the Royal Norwegian Air Force was the first plane to spot the *Tecumseh*. It had just enough time to radio its position when a missile from the *Tecumseh* blew it out of the sky.

The British destroyer *Formidable* was already on duty near the island, when it received a message from the Admiralty, directing it to head for the bay where the *Tecumseh was* spotted.

A similar message went out to the US *Patterson*, a guided-missile cruiser.

Both ships were in sight of one another when each was struck by missiles.

The *Formidable* blew apart amidship. Each section burned for a long time.

The *Patterson* became a floating inferno and ran aground.

There were no survivors from either ship.

At 0820 Boxer peered through the *Neptune*'s periscope and saw the wreckage of the two ships. The *Patterson* was still burning and the bow section of the *Formidable* was over on her side. He lowered the periscope and keyed the DO. "Make seven zero feet."

"Making seven zero feet," the DO responded.

Boxer keyed the FCO. "Activate ECM."

"ECM activated," the FCO answered.

Boxer walked to the chart table and studied the map of the island. The island was gray, barren rock. According to the chart, it was uninhabited. "The bay she's in is small," Boxer said. "There are several sand bars that would cover our approach... We may be able to get close enough for a short-run torpedo shot before she picks us up."

Boxer stood silent for a moment; then he made his decision and keying the forward torpedo room, he ordered all tubes armed with nuclear torpedoes.

"Arming tube one, two, three, and four with nuclear fish," the TO answered.

The COMMO keyed Boxer. "Admiral, a signal is coming in from Admiral Borodine."

"Roger that," Boxer answered. "Patch it through."

"*Novgorod* to *Neptune*. Please respond."

"Boxer here."

"We have the *Tecumseh* between us," Borodine said.

"There's nothing on the *Shark*. She still might be in the *Tecumseh*."

"She might… One of our fishing trawlers sighted her just before she entered the bay… She's riding low in the water," Borodine said.

"She might have filled the bay with water to fool us into thinking the *Shark* is still there," Boxer countered.

"Possibly… But we still have the *Tecumseh*."

"Coordinate with me," Boxer said.

"We will attack together," Borodine answered.

Boxer was about to agree, when the COMMO broke in and said, "Stand by, *Novgorod*… Stand by."

"Standing by," Borodine answered.

"Message coming in from headquarters," the COMMO said.

"Roger that," Boxer answered. "Put it through."

"Boxer, this is Kinkade… Trish died at five o'clock this morning… Given the circumstances, I thought you'd want to know."

Boxer's throat tightened, but he managed to clear it and answer, "Yes… Thank you."

"Good luck," Kinkade said, ending the conversation.

Boxer keyed the COMMO. "Patch Admiral Borodine through again," he said.

"Word about the *Shark*?" Borodine asked immediately.

"Trish died at five o'clock this morning," Boxer said, his voice tightening again.

"She was a lovely woman," Borodine answered after a long pause. "A very lovely woman."

Boxer uttered a deep sigh. "She's better off dead," he said. "Much better than to be a vegetable for the rest of her life."

"Yes," Borodine answered. "Yes… She's better off dead."

Boxer cleared his throat and forced his mind to concentrate on the immediate situation. There would be time enough later to think about Trish. "We will attack together," Boxer said.

"At oh nine one five," Borodine replied.

"Roger that," Boxer answered. "I will resume radio contact at oh nine one two."

"Roger that," Borodine answered. "Out."

Boxer switched off the mike and keyed the EO. "Flank speed," he said.

"Going to flank speed," the EO answered.

"Helmsman," Boxer said, "come to course two one degrees."

"Coming to course two one degrees," the helmsman answered.

"Get the DB," Boxer said to Riggs.

As soon as the DB reported, Boxer asked, "Any luck?"

"Negative, sir… No response from the *Shark*. If she's not in the *Tecumseh*, she could be out of range or shielded by one of the islands."

"Keep trying… We're going for the *Tecumseh*, but if you get the slightest hint that the *Shark* isn't in her, I'll break off… I don't want to risk this boat against a secondary target if I don't have to."

"Understood, sir," the DB answered.

Borodine watched the scopes as the survivors of the wolf pack moved as stealthily as possible toward the bay where the *Tecumseh* rode at anchor.

"I am sorry to hear of your friend's death," Viktor said, in a low voice.

Borodine nodded. He had told Viktor about his wild affair with Trish.

"Perhaps after this operation is over you and I may talk of her in some quiet place?" Viktor offered.

"I suspect that Boxer and his EXO will do the same thing," Borodine said; then he asked, "I wonder if he knew her as well as, and in the same way, that I did?"

Viktor shrugged. "I doubt if even she would be able to answer that."

"You're very wise, Viktor," Borodine said, "and my very good friend." He took a moment to blow his nose and clear his throat; then he said, "We have a battle to fight."

"A hard one," Viktor responded.

Borodine nodded and sounded general quarters. Then over the MC, he said, "All hands, battle stations... All hands, battle stations." He keyed the forward torpedo room. "Arm all tubes with nuclear fish."

"Arming all tubes with nuclear torpedoes," the TO answered.

Borodine keyed the EO. "Flank speed."

"Flank speed," the EO answered.

Borodine watched the instruments on the COMCOMP.

The SO keyed Borodine. "Admiral, I've got a bearing on the *Shark*."

Borodine checked the scope. The blip identified as the *Shark* was moving slowly to the northwest, not fifteen miles from his present position. "Have computers reconfirm," Borodine ordered.

The SO used the COMCOMP's subroutines to analyze the passive sonar trace from the target. "It's the *Shark*," the SO said, after a few tense seconds had passed.

"Damn, she's hardly moving," Viktor said.

Borodine rubbed his beard. "Do I contact Boxer, or do I let him attack the *Tecumseh*, while I go after the *Shark*?" he asked.

"By the time he joins us —" Viktor began.

"We must get the *Shark*," Borodine said. "Notify all boats to come to course two nine five degrees."

"Aye, aye," Viktor answered.

"Helmsman," Borodine said, "come to course two nine five degrees."

"Coming to course two nine five degrees," the helmsman answered.

After several minutes elapsed, Viktor said, "The slow speed is suspicious. She must know we're here."

"Let's trust the computers until we know differently," Borodine answered, realizing that Viktor was worried about being decoyed again by MAGPLATs.

Borodine keyed the forward torpedo room. "Disarm torpedoes in tubes one and two... Reload with nuclear SUBROCs."

The TO repeated the order.

A channel was opened to the other subs, allowing them to follow the attack.

Several minutes later the TO reported, "SUBROCs ready to launch."

"Fire one," Borodine said.

The launch sounded like a conventional torpedo. A few seconds later the solid fuel ignited. The missile fought its way to the surface atop a column of fire and steam that shoved it through the water. It broke surface at a shallow angle. In a matter of seconds it plunged into the ocean again, diving down to seek its target.

"She's in the water again, sir," the SO sang out.

Borodine switched on the MC. "All hands, rig for shock waves. Counting down." His eyes found the FC clock and he began counting. "Five ... four ... three ... two ... one... Mark!"

The *Novgorod* shuddered from the impact of the shock wave, her plates screamed as the boat was wrenched. Green lights on the console went to red.

"All section chiefs, report damage," Borodine said over the MC.

One by one the section heads reported, "No damage."

Borodine breathed a sigh of relief: the boat was secure.

"It couldn't have been that easy," Viktor said.

"Admiral, I've got another bearing on the *Shark*," the SO reported. "Fainter and farther away... Bearing two six degrees... Range, twenty thousand yards."

Borodine cursed and slammed his hand against his armrest. "Decoyed by a minisub or a MAGPLAT!"

The COMMO keyed Borodine. "In-coming message from Admiral Boxer," he said.

"Have him stand by," Borodine answered; then he keyed the forward torpedo room. "Launch SUBROC two."

"SUBROC two launched," the TO answered.

Borodine picked up the mike. "We've made a second ID of the *Shark* at a different location... We've launched another SUBROC. Probably neither target is the *Shark*. I will explain after the detonation." He abruptly broke the connection.

"Can we take another shock wave?" Viktor asked.

"We'll soon find out," Borodine answered and, switching on the MC, he said, "All hands, rig for shock wave… All hands, rig for shock wave."

The *Neptune* rolled violently in response to the second atomic blast and the thunderous sound hung in the confines of the steel hull for several long seconds.

Boxer wanted to speak to Borodine about what was happening, but he had gotten enough from Borodine's terse explanation to know that Bush had either decoyed them with automatically controlled minisubs or MAGPLATs. No matter which he had used, he had accomplished his purpose. He had confused his hunters by making them doubt everything their instruments were telling them. It was an absolutely brilliant ploy, even if it was conceived and executed by a madman.

"Admiral," the SO said, "I have the configuration of the bay on the scope."

Boxer checked the scope on the COMCOMP. The *Tecumseh* was riding at anchor in the center. She had already rewritten naval warfare by automatically defending herself against scores of air attacks.

Boxer moved aside to give Cowly a better view of the scope.

"Do you think the *Shark* is still in the *T*?" he asked.

"No," Boxer said quietly. "But even if she isn't, she must be destroyed. Bush has made it impossible for her to remain afloat."

"She was a good ship," Cowly commented wistfully.

"A very good one," Boxer agreed and continued to study the sonar display. He had a bad feeling about the operation, but he was determined to carry out his original plan. He desperately hoped that one of the targets destroyed by Borodine was the *Shark*. And if not that, he hoped the *Shark* still lay within the

Tecumseh. And if not, that some ship or plane of the Russian Northern Fleet would stop the *Shark* before it launched its missiles.

The SO keyed Boxer. "Sandbank ahead, Admiral. But no channel."

Boxer gave his full attention to the scope in front of him. "Roger that," he answered. The *Neptune* was at the entrance to the bay and slowly crawling her way forward, shielded from detection by the *Tecumseh* by sandbanks. But not from a MAGPLAT or a sonar buoy!

Boxer keyed the DO. "Diving planes up zero five degrees."

"Diving planes up zero five degrees," the DO answered.

Boxer keyed the EO. "Reduce speed to zero five knots."

"Reducing speed to zero five knots," the EO answered.

"Still not clearing," the SO reported.

Boxer ordered the DO to come up two zero feet.

"Coming up two zero feet," the DO replied.

"Not clearing," the SO said.

Boxer ordered a rise of another thirty feet.

"Clearing," the SO reported.

The *Neptune* passed over the sandbank, her propellers tearing into it and clouding the water.

"Target," the SO said. "Bearing, three two zero degrees... Range, three thousand yards."

At three thousand yards, Boxer and everyone aboard the *Neptune* knew that the explosion from a nuclear torpedo would destroy not only the *Tecumseh*, but also the *Neptune* and most of the island as well.

Boxer forced the consequences from his mind and keyed the forward torpedo room. "Load and arm —"

Suddenly the *Neptune* reeled violently. The explosion ripped the bow open, lifting it above the sandbank. Then the boat settled down into the sand and the stern came out of the water, its props spinning wildly above the surface of the water.

The bridge crew were thrown to the deck. They rolled forward when the bow sank.

Boxer grabbed onto the helmsman's chair and hauled himself into it. Then he fought his way up the sloping deck to the COMCOMP and threw the master switch, shutting down the nuclear power plant and the engine.

"Forward torpedo room gone," the DCO said. "Hull ruptured."

"Casualties?" Boxer asked.

"Twenty dead... Eight wounded," Riggs answered.

"Roger that," Boxer answered and said calmly, "All hands, abandon ship... All hands, abandon ship... Abandon ship... Abandon ship... Cowly, take them out through the sail."

"Aye, aye, skipper," Cowly answered.

Confusion was held to a minimum though many of the injured were bleeding profusely.

Boxer continued to monitor communications.

"Time to go, Admiral," Riggs said, putting his hand on Boxer's shoulder.

Boxer nodded, left the COMCOMP and went up the ladder. Riggs was behind him. He would be the last to leave the boat.

A second explosion impacted below the water level a moment after Boxer jumped into a rubber raft with Cowly, the DB, and some of the others.

Flames leaped from the open hatch. Riggs began to scream. The DB started back toward the hatch.

"Nothing you can do," Boxer said, grabbing hold of him by the arm. "Sit down. That's an order, sailor."

The DB dropped back to the bottom of the raft.

Boxer grabbed a plastic oar and began to paddle with the rest.

Across the bay, the long, low hull of the *Tecumseh* lay at anchor. Even though she was burning now, she was still fighting off her attackers.

"Head for that beach," Boxer said, pointing with his oar to a gravelly gray beach some three hundred yards off. It was the nearest spot they'd be able to land and a low, rocky ridge would give them some cover from the *Tecumseh* and, when night fell, from the wind.

Suddenly a F16 came roaring in off their port side and the water was stitched with machine-gun slugs. Boxer went over the side. There was no time to look back to see if the others had done the same. The gray water was freezing. He started to swim but knew he wasn't going to reach the beach.

Happy moved toward the sinking man. Acting on an instinct older than the commands programmed into him by his trainer, he lifted the man toward the surface; then he pushed the man's head out of the water, not knowing why. He only knew that it would mean death for a man to sink below the surface of the water. He continued to move the man toward the beach, where he knew there were others of his kind.

Cowly and the others were huddled, shivering on the gravel beach below the cliffs when the dolphin rolled Boxer onto it.

All of them stood there unbelieving until the SO said, "This can't be happening. That's a man."

Cowly's voice broke as he yelled, "Boxer!" He ran into the water up to his knees and dragged Boxer by the arms to the shore.

The dolphin chirped, turned, swam out a short way and dove, heading toward the supership he had already identified.

"He's not breathing," Cowly shouted to the others and, straddling Boxer's chest, he began to give him CPR. The others gathered around him.

After a few minutes, Boxer's eyelids began to flutter. He started to cough.

Cowly rolled him over and he coughed out a lot of water.

"Didn't think I'd make it," Boxer sputtered. "Went down for the count."

"Almost didn't make it, skipper," Cowly said. "A dolphin brought you to the beach."

Boxer rolled onto his back and pulled himself up into a sitting position. He took several deep breaths and looked at the men around him. Besides Cowly and the DB, there was only the SO and a cook. "One of our planes shot us up. I went into the water and I started to swim; then I became too tired to continue and I felt myself going down. The rest of it —" He shook his head and, looking up at Cowly, he said, "It had something to do with Trish, with Borodine. It was very strange; then I felt something take hold of me."

"The dolphin," the DB said. "He brought you ashore."

Boxer raised his eyebrows.

"He did, skipper," Cowly said.

Suddenly a Phantom streaked toward the *Tecumseh* and released its missiles. In an instant the plane and the missiles streaking out in front of it became balls of fire.

"Christ," the SO swore. "Nothing can get close to that damn ship."

"We better get out of here before we're spotted and the beach is raked from the *T* or from one of our planes," Cowly said.

"Behind those boulders," Boxer said, pointing to several huge rocks midway between the water and the cliffs.

"Let me help you," Cowly offered.

"I can manage," Boxer said. "I'll bring up the rear. The rest of you go."

Led by Cowly, the men ran, zigzagging to the boulders.

Boxer followed. Every part of him ached, but he pushed himself until, panting, he dropped next to Cowly.

In the war room below the White House, Stark, Kinkade, and the full cabinet looked up at the huge monitor. For the past several hours they had been watching the progress of the battle via Argos-Four, a spy satellite hurled into stationary orbit five hundred miles above the North Pole several hours before.

"The Russians hold everything," Kinkade said. "They're even looking at the same picture that we are."

"They have more to lose than we do," the President answered.

"According to all the reports our nearest submarine," Stark said, "is fifty nautical miles away. The *Neptune* was —" He stopped. The loss of the *Neptune* shook him. He cleared his throat and continued. "That's an hour away at best. I have already ordered it to the island."

"In an hour it could be all over," Kinkade said sourly.

No one in the room was willing to challenge the comment.

Happy had identified the *Tecumseh* before he pushed the man onto the beach, and hoping his trainer would reward him with shrimp, he swam toward the *Tecumseh*.

His powerful tail propelled his streamlined body close to the hull of the ship. He bounced his sonar against the ship's keel, checking its configuration by sound. He located the stabilizer fins: their design matched the image in his memory. He had found it!

Expecting to be rewarded by buckets of shrimp, he swam rapidly around the ship several times. Plastic feelers protruded from the packets strapped to his back. At the base of the feelers were nonmetallic trigger mechanisms undetected by the *Tecumseh*'s electronic senses. And to the ship's sonar, Happy was just another big fish.

Happy swam back, just in time as the *Tecumseh* exploded.

"That came from the *T*!" Cowly said, pulling himself up to get a better look. "She's settling by the stern."

Boxer scrambled to his feet and looked out into the bay.

Another explosion at the stern sent a rush of black smoke into the air.

Suddenly a Russian Backfire came roaring in from the east and fired a salvo of three missiles. The three missiles struck the *Tecumseh* amidship and the entire side of the ship disintegrated in a sheet of white flames.

An instant later another explosion broke the *Tecumseh* in half. She was dead!

Within minutes, British and Danish helicopters were circling the *Tecumseh*'s carcass like flies, unafraid that some nervous twitch of the dead beast might destroy them.

"The UWIS will protect us," muttered Bush, his head cocked at an odd angle. "It can see every bit of sea floor for better than twenty miles around. Every particle, you understand. Every starfish. Every grain of sand."

"Interesting," McElroy answered, trying to keep calm, though he knew that Bush was insane. He was seated in a chair opposite Bush.

"I'll activate it," Bush said, sitting down at the COMCOMP.

McElroy saw what appeared to be a video picture of the sea. "Where are we?" he asked.

"In the center of the abyssal plain of the Norwegian Sea. If you want a thrill, look at the depth gauge." Bush pointed to it. "Three thousand five hundred feet. This is the deepest we can go. They'll have trouble finding us at this depth. Even the Russian killer darts will have trouble finding us. They work best at short range. Range... You ever hear that song 'Home on the Range'?"

"Sure, when I was a boy."

"I lived on a farm when I was a kid. There was lots of horses. I always liked horses, because of their eyes I think. Their big deep eyes." His eyelids fluttered. He seemed ready to collapse, but by sheer force of will straightened up again.

"What about the horses?" McElroy asked, wanting to keep him talking.

"What? What horses?"

"Never mind," McElroy answered and, realizing he was hungry, said as much.

Bush glared at him. "I bet you are."

"Huh?"

"Do you think I haven't figured out that you've poisoned the food? That's why you haven't eaten. Now you're trying to tempt me, but it won't work."

"Why would I want to do that? I don't know how to drive this sub. You're the only one who can do that."

Bush sneered and pointed the gun at McElroy again. "You must take me for a fool, you stupid traitor! I know your friends are aboard waiting for me to drop. I can hear them in the air shafts, lurking in the storage lockers. Because I've got you, they don't dare rush me. So just walk easy! I'm not afraid of them; but the instant I see them coming, you're dead meat. Understand?" His eyes narrowed to slits and he said craftily, "And don't think you've been able to keep your talks with NATO a secret from me. I know all about them."

"My what?" McElroy asked. He was terrified now. Bush was getting worse and there was nothing he could do about it.

"Your secret radio to headquarters — I've heard it; oh yes, I've heard it. The radio you use to tap my thoughts. But it works both ways," he grinned. "You forgot that, didn't you. I listen to your transmissions. You think you can stop me from firing the missiles, but you can't. No one can. I've got a plan."

"Bush, remember our mission," McElroy pleaded. "Believe me, I'm with you, not against you. Remember the plans we made? Remember how it is going to be? The democracies — galvanized into action. The Soviet giant on its knees. The giant falls; its head struck off. And we'll be there — just the two of us — to take over the reins of government."

"Yes, heads will roll," Bush said. "On both sides." Then he made half a turn and keyed commands into the COMCOMP, while keeping a close watch on McElroy. "I'm turning back."

"You can't do that!"

Bush laughed mirthlessly. "I have a new plan and new targets. I'll show you." He keyed another command and the FC monitor lit up with a list of targets that included mostly Russian cities, but also Washington, London, Paris, and several more.

"You can't do that," McElroy shouted. "It's not the plan. You can't blow up half the world just to —" He saw Bush's trigger finger tighten and he dropped to the deck.

The bullet smashed into a control panel, shorting out several instruments.

McElroy scrambled to his feet.

Bush squeezed off another round.

A searing pain slashed across McElroy's shoulder, but he kept moving. He flung himself on Bush and, grabbing him by the throat with one hand, he slammed him in the face with the other.

Bush tried to club his attacker.

McElroy kneed him in the groin.

Gagging, Bush slumped to the floor and held the gun loosely.

McElroy glanced at the UWIS. They were heading back toward Iceland and the combined fleets of the most powerful countries in the world. He looked down at Bush and began to sweat.

Boxer, Cowly, and the other three men stood on the beach and watched the *Tecumseh* burn; then suddenly a British Sea King helicopter swooped toward them and over the loudspeaker system, the pilot said, "Stand where you are. If you attempt to run, you will be killed."

"Everyone, freeze!" Boxer ordered.

An instant later, a dozen heavily armed Royal Marines jumped from the hovering craft and surrounded them.

It took Boxer three minutes to convince the lieutenant in charge that he was Admiral Jack Boxer of the U.S. Navy and that the men with him were, like himself, survivors of the *Neptune*.

And five minutes later, Boxer and Cowly led a search party of marines aboard what was left of the *Tecumseh*. The *Shark* was not part of the wreckage and the bodies they found were burned beyond recognition.

"She was a good ship," Boxer commented when they were topside again. "And manned by good men."

Cowly agreed, pointing to the sail of a Russian attack submarine that was just breaking water about two hundred yards away.

"You have a call, Admiral," a marine communicator said, handing Boxer a radio the size of a cigarette pack.

"If it was any smaller, it wouldn't be," Boxer said.

"The next model is half the size of that one," the marine said.

Boxer nodded, keyed the radio, and identified himself.

"Comrade Admiral," Borodine said, "will you please come aboard the *Novgorod*? I will send a launch for you."

"It's the best offer I've had all day," Boxer answered. "But I need a set of dry, clean clothes."

"That can be arranged," Borodine answered with a laugh.

"Out," Boxer answered, as he watched a small boat detach itself from a depression in the submarine's hull. A powerful inboard quickly propelled it between the two vessels. As soon as it came alongside, two of the marines lowered a rope and the bubble top on the boat slid back.

Boxer thanked the Royal Marine lieutenant and went over the side, carefully making his way down the rope. When he reached the deck, he was saluted by two Russian sailors. He returned the salute.

One of the sailors gestured him inside the bubble. Boxer nodded and sat down. The second sailor joined them and took his place at the controls. The roof slid back into place and the boat sped away.

Several minutes later, the boat became part of the submarine's hull; the top slid back and the three of them entered the *Novgorod* through an airlock.

When Boxer lifted his head after ducking through the bulkhead door, he saw Borodine standing there.

Wordlessly they shook hands.

A man came toward them and took his position next to Borodine, who jerked his thumb at him. "Comrade Captain, Lieutenant Grotkin, political officer aboard the *Novgorod*. He is filing an official protest over your presence on this boat."

"Official protest, eh," Boxer said, saluting the man, "now why would he want to do something like that?"

Grotkin returned the salute. "You have no right —"

"Not now," Borodine told him. "We have more important matters to attend to. Admiral, will you please follow me to the wardroom."

"Wait," Grotkin said. "I told you to blindfold him first."

Borodine ignored him and turned.

Boxer followed.

"I will report this breach of security to the highest authority," called Grotkin after them.

Borodine stopped and turned, "If the highest authority survives the *Shark*'s missiles, I will willingly answer the charges. If not —" He shrugged and continued on his way.

All of the boat's officers were in the wardroom and Borodine introduced Boxer to all of them. When he came to Viktor, he said, "This one you already know."

Boxer nodded and quickly realized that Viktor had been promoted to the rank of captain first class. He shook his hand and said, "It seems we've all been promoted. Do you think that it might be a conspiracy between our governments?"

"If it is," Viktor answered, "I am in favor of it."

Boxer looked at Borodine. "I'm in favor of it too. What about you?"

"Certainly," Borodine answered.

When the introductions were over, Borodine called his officers to attention and, facing Boxer, he said, "I and my crew salute the men who were aboard the *Neptune*. This time we are brothers in arms against a common enemy. To you and your men." Borodine's hand came up in a smart salute.

"On behalf of my men living and dead, I accept your salute," Boxer answered, returning the courtesy to Borodine.

With the exception of Viktor and Grotkin, the other officers returned to their duties.

Borodine took out a pack of American cigarettes and offered one to Boxer. "Something I brought from the States," he said, holding a lighter out to Boxer and then lighting his own cigarette. "You still make good cigarettes."

Boxer nodded and blew smoke through his nose.

"Our Northern Fleet has detected what was probably the *Shark* slipping through our SOSUS net near the Arctic Circle. But its speed and its depth were so great it got past even as the data was being analyzed. Having hunted for the *Shark* myself on several occasions, I know how difficult it is to find her, much less destroy her. But we must do both."

Boxer nodded.

"If she moves farther north," Viktor said, "pack ice in some places will hamper ASW efforts. And once she reaches the Barents Sea, the shallow bottom makes the usual long-range ASW activity very, very difficult."

"I'll save you the trouble of asking me," Boxer said. "I'll go."

Borodine grinned. "Good. Very good," he said, slapping Boxer on the back. "I didn't think you'd refuse."

"But I have one request," Boxer told him. "I want to bring my EXO and an enlisted technician along."

"Out of the question!" Grotkin exclaimed.

"Why do you need them?" Borodine asked.

"Cowly knows the *Shark* as well as I do. That means you'll have two experts to help you find and kill the *Shark*."

Borodine nodded.

"And as for the technician," Boxer explained, "he may be our only real chance to get the *Shark*. He's trying to figure out a way to enter the *Shark*'s computers and take control of her."

"Call your men aboard," Borodine said. "We leave at once." Then to Viktor he said, "See that Comrade Admiral Boxer and the men coming aboard are provided with clean clothing and whatever else they may need."

"Aye, aye," Viktor answered with a gleam in his eyes.

Borodine looked at Boxer. "After the battle we will talk — there are things that must be said — but now we must first find and then destroy the *Shark*."

"Let's hope lady luck is on our side," Boxer answered, "because we're going to need all the help she can give." There was no need to say any more. He knew that Borodine understood just how formidable a weapon system the *Shark* was.

Borodine nodded and said, "I would even use prayer if I thought it would help." Then he keyed the duty officer: "Stand by to get under way in fifteen minutes."

"Aye, aye, Comrade Admiral," the duty officer answered.

A NOTE TO THE READER

Dear Reader,

If you have enjoyed the novel enough to leave a review on **Amazon** and **Goodreads**, then we would be truly grateful.

Sapere Books

Sapere Books is an exciting new publisher of brilliant fiction and popular history.

To find out more about our latest releases and our monthly bargain books visit our website:
saperebooks.com